NURSE AT SMOKY RIVER

Nurse At Smoky River

by
Denise Conway

Dales Large Print Books
Long Preston, North Yorkshire,
England.

British Library Cataloguing in Publication Data.

Conway, Denise
    Nurse at Smoky River.

A catalogue record for this book is
available from the British Library

ISBN 1-85389-967-4 pbk

First published in Great Britain by Robert Hale & Company,
1974

Cover illustration © Viney by arrangement with P.W.A.
International Ltd.

The moral right of the author has been asserted

Published in Large Print 1999 by arrangement with Robert
Hale Ltd.

C40345430Z

Dales Large Print is an imprint of
Library Magna Books Ltd.
Printed and bound in Great Britain by
T.J. International Ltd., Cornwall, PL28 8RW.

CHAPTER ONE

Brian Atkinson sprinted up the steps to the door which gave access to a large block of offices in down-town Vancouver and showed no surprise when it opened after a slight push. He often arrived early in the morning to catch up with the accumulation of work. Although it was not yet eight o'clock the janitor was polishing the tables in a side interview room.

Brian nodded to the man, stepped into a lift and pressed the button for the fourth floor. Alighting there he walked rapidly down the corridor then stopped abruptly when he noticed a girl leaning against the door of his suite of offices. She wore a nurse's uniform and was without a coat. Her face, a very attractive one, he thought, was pale and tired.

'Say, is anything wrong?' he enquired anxiously as he moved towards her. It was so unusual to find a nurse outside the Cree Oil Company Office especially at this hour in the morning!

She straightened and smiled a little nervously. 'No. I came early because I wanted to apply for the post as soon as possible.'

He smiled. 'You sure you're in the right place? This isn't an employment bureau.'

'I know.' She glanced at the letters in gold on the door. 'I was told to come here.'

He looked intrigued then pulled his key-ring from his pocket, selected one and opened the door. 'Come right in, Nurse. My room is through here.'

The girl followed him into the inner office and sat down in the chair he indicated she should use. She glanced swiftly around then with hands folded in her lap, her back straight, she waited for him to open the interview.

'Now you can enlighten me,' he said quietly, looking at her curiously across his desk. 'I guess it's urgent otherwise you wouldn't have come at this hour.'

'Yes.' She spoke slowly and distinctly as if a little afraid. 'It's very important. I'm nursing at the General Hospital. I came off duty at six and came straight over.'

'You waited outside the building? I'm sure the doors weren't open then.'

She smiled faintly. 'It was of no consequence. I'm seeing you now. I'm very grateful.'

'For what?' He frowned. 'I can't see how I can help!'

She leaned forward and said eagerly. 'I was told you employ doctors and nurses in your oil camps in Alberta.'

He chuckled. 'Obviously you have no idea of the immensity of the place or the kind of work it is! We do have many fields; an extraction plant at Athabasca sands, that's still in the experimental stage, several in the Peace River area and a few

9

others west. I don't recollect having a single doctor or nurse at any of them. Most of them have hospitals in adjoining towns.'

She looked disappointed. 'This appointment is somewhere near the Peace River. My brother and fiancé are working up there. I haven't heard from them for some time and I'm anxious about them. It would be marvellous if I could see them even for a short time. A nurse I'm working with mentioned that she knew the doctor who is at the same camp and she believed that his assistant was leaving soon. I was hoping I could be the replacement.'

Atkinson smiled disbelievingly. 'You do understand the nature of the territory? Some of it is pure wilderness, real exciting for game hunters but scarcely the place for a young lady. You can travel for miles without finding a settlement.'

'Yes I know. I wouldn't mind that. I'm prepared to rough it.'

'Hmm. Perhaps it would be as well to

tell me your name.'

'June Bentley. I'm fully qualified.'

He smiled. 'I'm not the person you need. I don't normally deal with staff matters. But I will make a note of your application and hand it to my colleague when he comes in.'

'Thank you.' She hesitated then said quickly, 'You will let me know soon.'

'Don't be too hopeful! Your informant may be mistaken or the position may have been filled.'

She stood up. 'Thanks for seeing me. It was kind of you.'

'My pleasure,' he said smilingly. 'You go along and have some sleep. You look as if you could do with it.'

She smiled faintly. 'We had a hectic night; accident cases mostly. It goes like that sometimes.'

By nine o'clock the rest of the staff had arrived. Brian's co-partner Guy Burleigh raised his eyebrows enquiringly as he sat down at his desk.

'Couldn't you sleep? How long have you been here?'

Brian grinned. 'I met a real peach. She was waiting for me outside our door dressed in a nurse's uniform.'

'A nurse!' Guy looked astonished. 'Someone taken ill?'

'No. She came to ask for an appointment.'

'She came to the wrong place naturally.'

'I guess not. Have you a vacancy for a nurse in the Peace River district?'

Guy frowned. 'A guy sent in his resignation at Smoky River camp. That's the only one near there. It's real rugged. What she want to go there for?'

'She said she has a brother and a fiancé in our employ there. Name would be Bentley. Does that ring a bell?'

'No. We employ so many men. Give me a minute. I will ask Mary to look up the file.'

He was smiling when he returned. 'I've got it taped now. We do need a nurse but not a female one! Harley Tretton is the doctor at Smoky River Camp and he absolutely refuses to have a woman on the site. The girl was right. Her brother is working there. Damn fine engineer he is too!'

'Couldn't you give the girl a break? She sure was keen to go.'

'What's she like?'

'Lovely! Auburn hair, blue eyes with long dark lashes, unusual with that colouring, shapely legs and a wonderful smile.'

Guy grinned. 'Her work, you dope!'

'I didn't get that far.'

'That figures,' Guy said dryly.

Brian smiled. 'Wait until you've seen her!'

'I'm not likely to. I couldn't send a girl up there.'

'Why not? You need a replacement.'

'Sure.' Guy glanced at him doubtfully. 'You've never met Tretton have you? I pity the girl if we did send her.' He broke off and chuckled. 'I would give my next bonus to see his face if she did go. He'd be livid!'

'I doubt that, not once he's seen her. Anyway she has a fiancé to look after her.'

'It could make a difference I guess, with any other man. But Tretton took the post to get away from women. He was let down by the girl he hoped to marry. A week before the wedding she went off with another man taking Tretton's savings with her.'

'Nasty experience. No wonder he dislikes women! But he's been there some time according to this file. He ought to have got over it by now.'

'Maybe.' Guy looked thoughtful. 'As a matter of fact it's not easy to get a young man to work up there. None of his assistants have stayed long. It's too remote. Okay for a short spell but men need a change of scene. I'm real surprised that Tretton has stuck it so long. Seeing you're so keen on giving the girl a chance

14

I will find out from the hospital what her record is like.'

'Okay. That's fair enough. Now I have to get on. A lot of good arriving early has done me this morning!'

A few days later June was summoned to the phone. It was an outside call and she guessed before she picked up the receiver whom it might be. She had no friends except amongst the hospital staff for she had been in Canada only a little over three months.

'Nurse Bentley speaking,' she said nervously.

'This is Guy Burleigh, Cree Oil Company. Sorry I missed you nurse. I understand you applied for a position on our staff.'

'Yes, I did. Have I a chance?'

'That's up to you. The post is yours if you want it, nurse assistant at Smoky River Camp. Your brother is there. I checked.'

'That's wonderful!' June said breathlessly. 'Thanks very much! When can I start? And how do I get there?'

Guy chuckled. 'You sound keen! You will have to fly. There's no other way. It's in the heart of the bush. Call in and see me when it's convenient. I can give you the details then.'

She was silent for a second or two then asked anxiously, 'Will the plane fare be expensive?'

'It won't cost you a bean. The company will pay your expenses. Just let me know when you are free. We will arrange the flight.'

When June boarded the plane which was to take her to northern Alberta, she found that Guy Burleigh was with the men who were to accompany her.

He grinned at her as she took the seat next to him. 'It's nearly time for my supervisory check on Smoky River Camp. I thought I might as well go along and introduce you; oil the wheels as it were.'

June smiled at him gratefully not having the faintest idea why he had decided to go with her. If she had known that he was anticipating the aggravation which her arrival would bring to the Doctor in charge she would not have felt at all easy in her mind; might indeed have refused to go.

The passengers were a mixed bunch; young and middle-aged men in their twenties, thirties and forties. And when she listened to them talking she found that there were Poles, Ukrainians, French and Chinese with only three Canadians. The bush pilot had raised his eyebrows when he first caught sight of June but had made no comment thinking it wiser to hold his tongue with one of the Partners on board. The men seemed to be from all walks of life, students with longish hair, tough looking oil-men and a few city types.

'How long will it take us?' June asked Guy who had been watching with amusement the way she was eyeing the passengers.

'Normally about three hours but today

we are touching down at Grande Prairie so it will be longer.'

'Oh, why is that?'

'Some of the men have been detailed for Wapiti River. We are setting up a new section. They will be working on the seismograph rig. There's about a hundred men there camping in the bush.'

After that June relapsed into silence. Although Guy was pleasant enough she had not taken to him. She thought he was too dictatorial for a man of thirty-five. He was of medium build, had thin features and hard blue eyes beneath a narrow forehead heightened by thinning light brown hair. From the way the other passengers had greeted him, civilly but without warmth, she gathered that he was not too popular. The oil-men knew him well judging by the remarks about the camp they were going to. From time to time, these men eyed June askance and refrained from speaking to her. So she was grateful when the bush pilot winked at her as he helped her alight at Grande Prairie. They had a hot meal there whilst the plane was refuelled then flew off again half an hour later without the city types and students who had wandered off to find transport to the Wapiti River.

The grass land with woods of poplar was giving way to vast forests of larch, spruce and cotton-wood patched by huge squares of open farm land where the timber had been felled.

'Not many lakes up here,' Guy remarked. 'Drinking water can be a problem on some of the homesteads. We shall be over the Birch Hills in a moment and nearing the end of our journey. Smoky River is a tributary of the Peace and breaks away a little north of here.'

Not long after he had spoken June saw the roofs of wooden shacks, log cabins and a larger building which looked rather like a church. All were ringed with larch and spruce trees but beyond the circle to the north was a flat field stripped of the bush ready for the plane to make a landing.

With a confused vision of oil derricks, forests of fir and the outline of wooded mountains not far off, June straightened her starched cap and gripped her small case. The plane had left so early in the morning that she had not had time to change out of her uniform after she had come off duty, her last at the General Hospital. She had collected her luggage, said farewell to her friends and stepped into the cab that was waiting to rush her to the airport.

But now that she had practically arrived at her destination she was beginning to have doubts. She had not had time to write to Chris or her brother, Andrew. Everything had happened so swiftly. It had been a sudden impulse to join them and now she wondered whether they were going to be pleased to see her.

It's only because I'm tired, she thought. I wouldn't be thinking like this if I had had some sleep. Usually I've had four or five hours by now. And all the excitement has made my head ache. Being surrounded by men hasn't helped. I do hope there are one or two women in the camp.

She had little time after that for conjecturing. The plane had landed and the passengers were climbing out stiffly. The pilot gave June a hand down, pressing her hand and smiling warmly. Looking at him more closely she was surprised to see he was so young.

'Okay nurse? Watch yourself with the oil-men. Some of them don't know how to treat a lady. If you have any trouble let me know. I shall be only too pleased to help. I fly in every two weeks.'

She did not have time to thank him. Guy took her arm, nodded to the pilot and said curtly, 'No need for you to concern yourself. I can look after Nurse Bentley.'

Casting a swift glance at Guy as she walked beside him over the well-trodden grass track June wondered why he was smiling so broadly. And it was only when they had to push their way through groups of men that she began to understand. As the men fell away to allow them to pass their faces dropped and their tongues were stilled. June thought that she had never seen so many gaping mouths before.

'What's wrong with them?' she whispered keeping her eyes on the track.

Guy chuckled. 'They weren't expecting a female nurse. You've given them a shock.'

'Haven't they ever had a woman nurse in this camp?'

'No. Doctor Tretton won't have them.'

June stopped and looked at him doubtfully. 'Then why have you brought me here?'

'We thought that Tretton had had his own way far too long.'

She stared at him aghast. 'He doesn't know I'm coming?'

'I didn't see any reason to tell him. He's been informed that a replacement is arriving that's all.'

'You ought to have told me.'

'Would it have made any difference?'

'I wouldn't have come.'

'But you were so eager. You asked for the position and you knew you were replacing a male nurse.'

June looked at him unhappily. 'I wasn't to know that the doctor objected to women nurses.'

'He has to accept whom we send. Come on Nurse Bentley! I haven't got all day. It's too late now to change your mind. It would inconvenience everyone.'

She moved on reluctantly forgetting her qualms that her brother and fiancé might not want her there. A far greater obstacle was occupying her thoughts. What was Doctor Tretton like? she asked herself fearfully. Would he be very unpleasant?

Feeling miserably uncertain and keeping close to Guy she penetrated the circle of tall trees and emerged on to a dusty wooden sidewalk. It had been roughly made to keep the mud at bay when it rained and to mark out the dirt road which had been cut through the camp. The planks were so uneven that June found them dangerous to walk over, and after stumbling a few times she joined Guy on the road. It seemed an awful distance to the camp and June's eyes began to ache from gazing at the avenue of spruce whose columns seemed to be without end. The sun was hot and dazzling and after a few minutes she was wishing she had something cooler on. Her uniform felt tight and stiff ridiculously unsuitable for the trek she was making. Guy did not seem at all concerned about her but strode along rapidly fully preoccupied with his own thoughts.

Then suddenly the road widened into a large clearing. Log cabins and larger wooden shacks dotted the dusty road where men in chequered shirts paused to gape at June and Guy. One man put down the pail of water he was carrying so that he could indulge his mirth without drenching himself. June was too hot and tired to care. After the disclosure Guy had made nothing seemed to matter except the necessity to brace herself for that first meeting with Doctor Tretton.

Guy's amused voice startled her, shattering her carefully guarded courage. 'News travels fast. Harley is waiting for us.'

June raised her head and stared at the tall man who was standing with feet astride a few yards ahead. She stopped conscious of a clamminess that was not due to the heat of the day. It was fear, a dreadful sickening fear because the man looked so angry. His eyes almost closed beneath his black frown. His bare muscular arms were folded across his blue shirt which flapped loosely over his white drill trousers. His hair was black and unruly, his face lean and formidable. June moved forward keeping her gaze on the building behind him for she was very much aware of the antagonism confronting them.

'I promised I would be right back with

a replacement, Harley,' Guy drawled, his hard blue eyes faintly malicious. 'This is Nurse Bentley. She has a fine record so I know you won't be disappointed.'

'Not more than I am right now,' Doctor Tretton replied curtly. He looked grimly at June who felt like a specimen on a slide unable to remove herself from his penetrating gaze.

A few seconds passed then he said gruffly, 'Go across to the Mission House, Nurse. There's coffee on the stove. Help yourself but don't make yourself too comfortable. I guess you won't be staying too long.' He turned his head to give Guy an accusing stare. 'I have things to say to Mr Burleigh which might shock your delicate ears.'

June hesitated then receiving a nod from Guy she began to walk away from them. She breathed a little more easily after that for she realized that the doctor's wrath was directed more at Guy than at herself. All the same she did not feel at all happy about the situation and thought it probable that she would have to go back with Guy.

'Do you have to get fired up like this?' Guy asked irritably his eyes on the men who had come to the doors of their cabins to watch, their faces curious and amused.

'Darn stupid of you, Guy,' Harley said vehemently. 'You knew I wouldn't have her.'

'It's not for you to say, Harley. You are employed by the company same as I am. We couldn't replace Jackson at such short notice. Nurse Bentley offered to come. You ought to be mighty grateful.'

'I'd rather do without assistance!'

'That's a foolish remark! You know you can't manage on your own. You've been asking for extra help as it is.'

'She can't stay!' Harley was white about the lips and his eyes were steely.

Guy laughed. 'I'm not taking her back! She's on our payroll now. You can please yourself whether you allow her to assist you. But here she stays working or not!'

'Then I resign right here and now!'

'Okay, resign but it will have to be after you've worked your full time. We have a contract, remember? You break that and I will personally see to it that you never obtain a similar position.'

'Damn you Burleigh! You're enjoying this aren't you?'

'It has its amusing angle. You're a fool Tretton. Any other man would appreciate being in your shoes. Where's your eyes, man? Nurse Bentley deserves some recognition. I could have chosen worse.'

'I came up here to get away from females. Trouble will come of this, I'm warning you Burleigh! We haven't one woman in this camp and that's how it ought to be. We have enough troubles without inflicting us with a female nurse! The men work hard, get paid and come and go as they wish. With that red-head turning up in unexpected places, how the dickens do you think I can protect her?'

Guy grinned. 'You will work something out. By the way she isn't without protectors. She has a brother and a fiancé working here. Andy Bentley is one of our ace men so don't upset him. Her fiancé is Chris Ferris.'

'Why the heck didn't you say so before?' Harley growled.

'I didn't think it would make that difference. You know Harley not every young woman is out to get her claws into you.'

Guy flinched at the anger in Harley's grey eyes and he stepped back quickly afraid of his wrathful figure.

'I apologize! I guess I ought not to have said that.'

'Forget it!' Harley said contemptuously. 'I've never had a good opinion of you, Burleigh, even less now.' He began to walk away only turning his head slightly to ask, 'Want some coffee?'

'Sure,' Guy drawled. 'I have to take my

leave of Nurse Bentley before I call on the crew foreman.'

'Jo Skinner isn't in camp. He's over at the new drilling rig. They've had an unexpected find. You will be sending more men up I guess. That's why I've been insisting on extra help. Our accident rate is real high I can tell you.'

'Nothing serious as yet.' Guy said carelessly.

'That's right. I want to keep it that way. Men become careless, especially when you send so many greenhorns up here.'

'Are you criticizing our policy now?' Guy asked sharply.

'Someone has to. A few youngsters we've patched up in the past could have been injured for life.'

'We train them before we send them here.'

'For not long enough evidently.'

'The company has to make a profit. We spend too much on the men's welfare as it is.'

'We could do with a small hospital. The area is developing so fast we won't be able to cope soon.'

'You know as well as I do that sometimes the oil doesn't last. Only after we have drilled can we be sure it's going to be enough to pay for the outlay. Build a settlement here now and it might be a ghost town within a year. We have to be mighty sure first.'

'Okay! I know all that. That's why you ought to appreciate what I'm doing.'

'We do. We may not always see eye to eye, Harley but we know what you're worth. You offered to resign just now but we both know you didn't mean it. You wouldn't give up so easily.'

Harley's smile was a little twisted. 'Because of a female, you mean? No you're right. A little red-head wouldn't make me budge. All the same I'm not saying I go along with her being here!'

31

June glanced at them doubtfully when they pushed open the door of the Mission House. She had been surprised to find when she entered that it had been skilfully turned into a waiting-room, small surgery and a fairly large clinic. A stove in the middle of the waiting-room was blazing with logs and the place smelt strongly of coffee. She had pulled the bubbling pot to the side of the stove then walked over to inspect the clinic. There she had taken a jug of milk from the refrigerator collected a cup from a wall cabinet and returned to the stove to pour herself some of the delicious smelling coffee. It had tasted bitter but was stimulating and she was feeling less uncomfortable than when she had landed.

'What do you think of the set-up, Nurse?' Guy looked at her enquiringly. 'Do you think you're going to fit in here?'

She flicked a swift glance at the Doctor noticed the wry twist of his lips and the glint in his eyes and said nervously, 'It would be a new experience but if Doctor Tretton objects I would rather go back with you.'

'That's not so easy. We've signed you on now. Don't let the Doctor's manner put you off. He's used to having a male assistant but I bet it won't be long before he's appreciating having someone more attractive to work with.'

'Spare us the slick remarks, Guy!' Harley said curtly. 'Nurse is embarrassed enough as it is.' He turned to gaze straight at June. 'It's up to you, Nurse Bentley. It's a rough life. Think you can stick it?'

'I don't like giving up before I've started. I made up my mind to come and it seems cowardly to return without giving it a try. Anyway I want to see my brother and fiancé whether I go or stay.'

'There will be no time for that if you return with me,' Guy said firmly. 'I'm leaving almost at once. Pour me a cup of that stringent stuff you're drinking and then I will be off.'

Harley smiled twistedly. 'Looks as if we're stuck with one another, Nurse.'

'There's no need to make it sound so awful,' she retorted defensively. 'How about giving each other a month's trial?'

'Excellent idea!' Guy smiled brightly at both of them. 'It will give me more time to find a substitute. That doesn't mean you have to leave then Nurse but if you do decide you can't stand the life, let me know. You can radio a message or give a note to the bush pilot. A plane comes in every two weeks.'

'Thanks Mr Burleigh.'

June moved away and sat down on one of the chairs leaving the two men to talk without being overheard. She was feeling very dispirited and only the thought of seeing Chris and Andy kept her from changing her mind and going back with Guy. At least I shall have two men I can rely on, she thought, eyeing the tall, broad-shouldered doctor with misgivings. It's not going to be very pleasant or easy working with a man who has made it so plain that he doesn't want me in the camp.

CHAPTER TWO

June was rinsing the cups at the washhand-basin in the clinic when Harley Tretton came in. He had gone to see Guy off and had taken his time over it. He appeared uneasy as he walked towards her and a little nervous herself June did not say anything.

'I shall have to fix you up with a room,' he said gruffly. 'There's one adjoining the clinic you can have. It will be adequate. You can wash in the clinic and use the stove for hot water and coffee.'

June turned to face him. 'Thank you Doctor Tretton. Is that where your assistant usually sleeps?'

'No. We have a cabin set aside for him. I thought you might feel safer here.'

'I don't want to alter anything. A cabin sounds fine.'

'I wasn't only thinking of you. The men might be embarrassed. I would prefer you to sleep here.'

June remained silent. The severe tone of his voice made it impossible for her to argue over it. He opened the door and went inside without asking her to follow him so she remained where she was. He was in there so long that she wondered what he was doing then when he did come out she realized that he had been gathering up his personal items. He had a blanket and sheets rolled up under one arm and carried a hold-all filled with books and other things.

'You will find clean sheets and blankets in the cupboard over there,' he said curtly. 'If you need anything else just ask. Is that all the luggage you have?' He nodded to her small valise.

'No. I have a case somewhere. The pilot took it from me before I left.'

'I guess one of the men brought it in. I will make enquiries.'

37

When he had gone June went into the room he had said could be hers. It was square with windows opposite the door. A small hospital bed had been pushed up against the wall and was stripped to the mattress. A bookcase and chair were the only items of furniture and the windows were bare of curtains.

I bet it's cold in winter, she thought as she eyed the wooden floor and stark white walls. But then I don't expect I shall be here that long. However did the doctor sleep on that bed! It looks small even for me. His feet must have jutted over the end. He's very tall. I ought to be grateful to him for letting me have the room but I would have felt happier in a cabin. He's made me feel a nuisance. I suppose he will sleep in the cabin. I bet he's annoyed. It must have been convenient being in the hospital or Mission House as he called it.

She went back to the clinic and took a couple of blankets, sheets and a pillowcase from the linen cupboard and returned to the room to make up the bed. She was tucking in the top blanket when she heard the clump of heavy boots and thinking that it might be a patient she walked quickly into the waiting-room.

A thick set man with a weather-beaten, lined face stood hesitantly by the stove. But when he saw June he grinned in a friendly manner.

'Doc asked me to bring your case over, Nurse,' he drawled eyeing her with interest.

'Thank you. That was kind of you.'

'Have you ever been this far north before, Nurse?'

'No. I haven't been in Canada long, Mr ...?'

'Aaron. Everyone calls me that.' He glanced down apologetically at his soiled trousers and heavy boots. 'Sorry about the noise. I reckon I startled you.'

She smiled. 'My brother is working somewhere in this camp. Do you know him? Andrew Bentley.'

'Sure do.' He grinned. 'Say now, ain't that something! Fancy you being Andy's sister.'

'Could you tell him I'm here?'

He shook his head regretfully. 'I reckon that might take time. He's out on the new rig, good few miles from here.'

'What about Chris Ferris? Do you know where he is?'

'He's with Andy's crew.'

'Oh,' June looked disappointed. 'Well, thanks anyway, Aaron. Perhaps I could make the trip myself.'

'Out of the question, Nurse Bentley!' It was Doctor Tretton's firm voice. He was at the door and had overheard her conversation. He strode across to them, nodded a dismissal to Aaron who went out looking perplexed.

'Why?' June asked rather rebelliously. 'There doesn't seem to be anything to do here.'

'There will be,' he replied grimly. 'Out-patients will be arriving in a few minutes.

Do you want something to eat before we start?'

'No thanks. I had a meal at Grande Prairie.'

'In that case I will show you where we keep the records. There aren't many so I expect them to be kept up to date and at hand in case I need them.'

'Are your patients all oil-men?'

'Most of them plus the seismograph boys but we haven't many of them now. We treat anyone who has a mind to look in. There are a few farmers, ranchers and tradespeople in the district but some of them have a forty mile trip to reach us so we don't see them that often. When it's urgent one of us goes to them.'

'What about transport?'

'We have a jeep. It cuts along pretty niftily.'

'No ambulance?'

'This isn't a hospital unfortunately. We have to use one of the trucks for accident cases.'

'Are there any women in camp?'

His grey eyes glinted. 'No. The farmers and ranchers have wives and daughters but as I said we rarely see them.' He smiled mockingly. 'Am I making you nervous?'

'No,' she said quickly. 'I only asked because I was curious about the patients.'

'Well now you know. How long have you been nursing?'

'Since I was eighteen.'

'Not long then,' he drawled eyeing her speculatively.

'Seven years. I'm twenty-five.'

'Is that a fact? You had me fooled. I guessed you'd be about nineteen or so.'

She flushed. 'They wouldn't have sent me if I had been that young.'

'Hmm. There's no telling what Guy will do.' He scowled darkly.

June moved to the desk at the far end of the room, opened the drawers systematically then walked into the clinic to look for a duster. As there did not appear to be any she found a suitable

42

rag and returned with that. Taking the contents from the drawers she began to dust the insides.

Harley watched her with a faint smile on his lips. 'That hasn't been done before,' he remarked.

'I thought not,' she replied. 'It's a pity to spoil such nice wood with fluff and dirt.'

'The wood was cut from a stand of cedar. One of the men made the desk for me. Please yourself about cleaning it. It won't make any difference. It needs to be polished.'

June pressed her lips firmly together and went on with the dusting. It was true that the insides of the drawers had been neglected for too long for there to be any improvement but at least she knew that they were cleaner. Also the activity gave her a sense of security.

Doctor Tretton disappeared into his sanctum and June sat down to wait for the patients. Luckily she was not idle for

43

long. Within a few minutes the waiting-room filled up and through the open door she could see a long line of men. Some of them had obviously jumped off the trucks bringing them back to camp only a few seconds before for they were dressed in their oil-rig clothes; heavy boots, shiny waterproof trousers and loose jackets. Their faces were streaked with dirt and oil and on their heads they had steel bowler hats also patched with mud and oil.

June stared at them in amazement. Surely they can't all be patients! she thought and beckoned for the first man to come back to the desk. She found his record card without difficulty for he had injured his fingers recently and had come for a new dressing.

June asked him to wait and took his card into the doctor.

'Your first patient, Doctor Tretton,' she said calmly as she placed the card on his desk.

He nodded. 'Shunt him in. He won't

take long. You can take him into the clinic after I've examined his hand and re-dress it if there aren't many waiting.'

'Not many waiting! Doctor, there are thirty or forty men out there. Goodness knows how long the queue is!'

He glanced up at her, his grey eyes grimly amused. 'Is that a fact?' he drawled. 'Wait in here, Nurse!'

He was gone only a few minutes and returned with a faint smile on his lips. 'Something I want you to do, Nurse Bentley,' he said brusquely.

'Yes, Doctor?' June gave him a curious look.

'Go out of here and walk slowly, extremely slowly through the Mission and don't stop until you come to the end of the line of men outside. Don't talk to them just turn round and walk back leisurely. I want them to have a good look at you.'

June stared at him in consternation. Her blue eyes were wide and indignant, her cheeks flaming. 'I can't do that!' she gasped.

'Sure you can,' he retorted. 'Go on. Get it over with. It will save us a lot of time. Once will be enough.'

'I should hope so!' She said almost bereft of breath.

'What's the matter? Haven't you seen a man before?' he jeered. 'Don't tell me you're scared!'

Her eyes flashed angrily. Then drawing herself up determinedly to her full height she turned her back on him and went through the door. He smiled sardonically as he followed and stood at the clinic door to watch her pass slowly through the waiting-room. All heads turned as she passed and whistles of appreciation followed her slender form. The cries increased as she disappeared from sight.

A few minutes later she returned. Her face was paper white, her eyes burning with anger revealing a challenge which silenced some of the men. She carried her auburn head high and keeping her emotion well under control she continued to walk slowly. Only afterwards did she realize the colossal effort it took. Reaching the men waiting by the desk she passed them without flinching then nodded to Doctor Tretton and followed him into his surgery.

Leaning against the door she had closed she said icily, 'Now, Doctor Tretton! Isn't it time we got down to something more important?'

He wiped the grin from his face and nodded. 'Sit down, Nurse, behind my desk. You can see to the patients I send in. I'm going to take your place outside. Anything serious you can't handle keep in reserve until I've finished.'

'It will take ages,' she protested.

'No, not long. Five or ten minutes at a guess.'

Much to her astonishment he was right. Once the men realized that June was not coming back they began to disappear.

And after five minutes only four men remained.

Harley went across to the door and bolted it then returned to his surgery. The room was empty but the door through to the clinic was open and he glanced inside. June was dressing the young man's hand her mind fully occupied with her task.

The patient was enjoying the unusual experience judging by the exaggerated groans which were prolonging the application of the new dressing. Harley frowned, pressed his lips firmly together and went in.

'There was no need for a complicated bandage, Nurse Bentley,' he said curtly.

'I did put another one on but he said it was too tight,' she said mildly. 'The hand is painful and he says he has to continue working. I thought the bandage would help to protect it.'

'He's never complained before. Off with you Harrison before I decide to take over.'

The young man got up quickly. 'Sure Doc. Nurse has done a fine job. Can I come back tomorrow?'

'That's not necessary. Next week unless you knock it or your arm swells.'

Harrison looked scared. 'It's not likely to do that, is it, Doc?'

June chuckled. 'There's very little wrong with it now. The dressing is merely to protect the newly formed skin.'

'I see.' The young man gave Harley an uneasy smile and sloped from the room.

Harley eyed June severely. 'You knew he was putting on an act.'

'Maybe.' She leaned down and began to collect the scissors and lint she had been using. And when she had put them in a drawer she straightened. 'They will soon get used to me. In time I shall be as familiar as the furniture.'

Harley raised his eyebrows at that but said nothing as he returned to his surgery. June hurried into the waiting-room to get the record card of the next patient. Half an hour later they were finished with the men.

'It wasn't so bad, was it?' Harley said giving her a faint smile.

'It was awful!' she retorted. 'I never guessed you could be so sadistic.'

'It worked didn't it? Could you have coped with all those men?'

'You know I couldn't. All the same I wouldn't go through that again.'

'You won't have to. They've all seen you now.' He took off his white coat. 'Make up the record cards. I've pinned a slip to each one. Then after you have tidied up you are free until tomorrow unless there's an emergency.'

'Do I prepare my own food?'

'No need for that. If you prefer to eat alone you can bring your meals back here. I do that sometimes if I'm in a hurry. There's a shack set aside as a dining hall.'

'Where did your previous assistant have his meals?'

'In the canteen with the men.'

'Then that's where I will eat,' she said matter of factly.

'Please yourself,' he said disinterestedly and turning his back on her he strode swiftly out of the Mission.

June found it pleasant working in the silence after the hectic activity she had become used to in a hospital. She took her time, stopping at frequent intervals to ask herself whether she would ever feel at ease with Doctor Tretton. She had never met anyone who made her feel so prickly. But to be honest he hadn't behaved too badly considering the way Guy had brought her here without consulting the doctor's wishes. Any man would be annoyed. All the same she felt a little suspicious of the derisive note in his voice at times and guessed that he was keeping his annoyance well under control. It might be better if he lost his temper and had it out with me, she mused. Then I should know where

I stand. It's the uncertainty which is so disturbing.

When she had finished the cards she went across to an open window and leaned out taking deep breaths of the sweet smelling air. She caught whiffs of the scent of pines and newly chopped wood mingled with wood smoke. The wind soughed through the trees around the camp now suffused with a crimson glow as the sun descended. A scratching noise startled her until she noticed a chipmunk searching for food and smiled to herself because it looked rather like an English squirrel. The difference so someone had told her was that the chipmunk lived in holes in the ground or in hollow logs and accumulated large stores of food which he tucked away in various places. It's not so very different here, she mused, gaining comfort from the small animal. I shall get used to it and perhaps in time the vastness won't be so frightening.

Doctor Tretton neglected to say what

time the evening meal is served, she thought. I feel awfully hungry. Surely it can't be much longer! She washed and changed into slacks and a white roll-neck sweater for she was beginning to feel cold. It was only the beginning of May and although the sun had been making the days unusually hot the mornings and evenings were chilly. A loud, booming sound warned her that supper was ready and she made haste to finish dressing. The gong was still being pounded as she crossed the rough ground, following the men who were strolling towards a narrow, rectangular shack where lights shone from the windows.

She climbed a few steps then panicked at the sight of so many men but because of the pressure from behind was forced to proceed. Then a man grabbed her arm and pulled her down to a vacant seat beside him.

'Sit here, Nurse,' he said eagerly, 'you will be able to get out more quickly.'

'Thanks.' Very embarrassed she glanced along the table and saw that all heads were turned in her direction. Then she noticed that the men had plates of food in front of them. Others who had been behind her were filing by a counter and calling out their orders to three men in white jackets and caps. 'Don't I have to order my meal first?' she asked in some bewilderment.

'I can get it for you. What would you like?'

'Same as you,' she replied quickly feeling uncomfortable at the attention. She had not had time to see what the men were eating and hoped that she had chosen something she liked.

The man came back with a huge steak, french fried potatoes and corn. It looked more than she could cope with but she thanked him and tucked in finding to her delight that it was delicious.

A man sitting opposite to her drawled, 'You gave us a mighty big surprise, Nurse. What made you join this outfit?'

She swallowed hastily and said, 'My brother Andy Bentley works here.'

'Is that a fact?'

'Yes. And I want to see as much of the country as I can. I haven't decided whether I want to stay for good.'

A man who had been eyeing her curiously suddenly spoke. He was not a Canadian although he had a faint accent. 'I guess you came from the same part of the world as me. How's London these days?'

She smiled. 'Progressing. I suppose my voice does give me away.'

'I'd sure like to get back there sometime. I've been in Alberta six years.'

'Do you like it?'

'Sure, nothing to grumble about. I reckon I know your brother. I've worked with his crew. Pity he's not here, he's way out in the bush.'

'How do they manage for sleeping quarters and food?'

In spite of the quantity of food Bill was consuming June noticed that he was slight in build with a thin face, dark hair and eyes and sallow complexion.

'They rig up tents and cook their own grub. Now that the site has developed I guess they've erected a few sheds. There's no hardship and they aren't away that long. Once they've checked the prospecting party's find they send for heavy equipment. Andy may come back before his crew gets the derrick up and probes the sub-strata.'

'I hope so.' June smiled. 'It will be good to see a familiar face.'

The man next to her chuckled. 'I reckon it took some nerve to face us. Don't let it throw you. We're not a bad bunch and Doc will keep an eye on you.'

'That's what I'm afraid of,' June said smiling faintly.

The men guffawed then talked amongst themselves. June took the opportunity to continue with her meal.

'Raisin or lemon pie?' Steve, the man at her elbow asked.

'Lemon but not too big a piece, please!'

'Okay. You needn't worry about the pastry. It's first class. One thing about this outfit, they feed you well.'

June glanced at Bill, the Londoner. 'Does Doctor Tretton eat with the men?'

He nodded. 'He's over there.'

June bent forward and looked towards the end of the table. Harley was deep in conversation with two men who were listening to him intently.

'Has he been here long?' she asked.

'Sure, ever since they opened up at Smoky River. That's about four years or more I guess.'

'He seems to get on well with the men.'

'He does his job. Some say he's too bossy but I've always found him a decent enough guy. Mind you he has to be tough. We get some queer blokes up here. A couple of years back we had a guy who tried to knife the Doc. The company got rid of him real fast I can tell you.'

'You trying to scare nurse away?' Steve

asked as he set a wedge of lemon meringue pie in front of June. 'You want coffee? I'll be back in a jiffy.'

'I'm giving him a lot of trouble,' June remarked eyeing Steve's broad figure as he pushed his way to the serving counter.

Bill grinned. 'He's the envy of all the blokes in the hut. They are all dying to do something for you.'

June smiled. 'I can't believe that.'

'Even a plain girl would cause a disturbance. You have stunned the lot but then I guess you know why. That's a gorgeous head of hair you have. Your cap hid most of it when you arrived.'

June chuckled. 'It's been a constant worry ever since I started nursing. Every matron I've worked under took exception to it. I never kept it covered up enough; it ought to be much shorter! One even went so far as to say that it disturbed the patients.'

Bill laughed. 'I bet!'

Steve returned with the coffee spilling it as he placed it on the table. The floor shook as he sat down.

'Hold on Steve!' Bill said. 'You will have the hut over.'

'I forget I'm such a heavy-weight,' the man said apologetically. 'Where I come from it's nothing unusual.'

Julie smiled at him. 'At a guess I would say that was Sweden.'

'That's right and real clever of you, Nurse.'

'Not really. You're so fair and those blue eyes give you away.'

'I bet he was a bonny baby,' Bill said cheekily.

Aware of Steve's red face June said quickly, 'Where do all these men work?'

'On derricks near the camp.' Steve had soon recovered. 'They had quite a find here four years ago. But it's beginning to peter out. That's why they've been prospecting for more sites.'

June felt a light touch on her arm and

glancing up saw the doctor standing there. 'You finished, Nurse? I will take you back to the Mission.'

She nodded and stood up. 'What time is breakfast, Bill?'

'Five thirty.' He grinned at her shocked expression. 'That's for the early shift. You can come in any time between six and nine.'

Harley said impatiently, 'Come along, Nurse!' And when the door had closed behind them went on irritably, 'There's no need to overdo it. Keep yourself aloof in future.'

'Why?' June asked bluntly. 'They were so friendly. It was kind of them to try and make me feel at ease.'

'Hmm.' He whipped a torch from his pocket and switched it on for the light was rapidly fading. 'Be careful of the ruts! I was giving you good advice, Nurse. If you become too friendly with one or two it will cause a heck of a lot of trouble with the others.'

'I don't agree. Any of them may need my help later on.'

'True but there's no need to stir up unnecessary commotion. I do know what I'm talking about. Some of these men have violent tempers.'

'I won't disturb the peace,' she said with a light laugh. 'Thanks for lighting the way, Doctor. I shall be all right now.'

'I'm coming in with you. You won't know where the lamp is.'

He went ahead shining the way with his torch and handed it over to her when they reached the clinic. She watched him light the lamp and carry it into her room and waited for him to leave after he had placed it on top of the bookcase. But he seemed in no hurry to go and was staring at the black expanse of bare window with a scowl on his face.

'We shall have to do something about that,' he muttered. 'I will nail a blanket up for tonight. Tomorrow we can fix up a rail.'

'Don't bother,' June said carelessly. 'I can undress in the dark.'

His black eyebrows lifted. 'What if there is a moon?'

She remained silent uncomfortably aware that whatever excuse she mentioned would be ruthlessly swept away. He had made up his mind that the window was to be covered.

'Keep the windows shut when the lamp is alight,' he instructed. 'Like most females I bet you take exception to flying creatures and I won't be around to answer your screams.'

'I can deal with them,' she replied stiffly.

He did not answer her and when she sent a swift enquiring glance in his direction saw that he was staring intently at her.

'Your hair ... it's too ...!'

'Too bright?' She was instantly on the defensive.

'If you like.' He stared at her accusingly. 'A camp full of men miles away from civilization and you have to turn up!'

She sighed. 'I thought we had dealt with that, Doctor Tretton. I'm a nurse not a cabaret girl. Surely that makes a difference! I have no wish to cause trouble.'

'You will, make no doubt about that!' He turned away. 'There's a hammer somewhere and a few nails. I was using them a few days ago.'

June sat down on the bed and waited for him to come back from the clinic. Then suddenly a noise at the window made her glance across there. Two faces were pressed against the glass, one bearded the other grotesquely twisted as he sniggered. She gasped and rising to her feet rushed into the clinic.

'For the love of Mike! What's the matter?' Harley asked sharply. 'You nearly had me over!'

'Nothing. I'm sorry. I came to see if I could help.'

'You seem mighty anxious all of a

sudden,' he said suspiciously. 'What happened?'

'Nothing.'

He dumped a red blanket on the floor and glanced out of the window. 'Did something out there disturb you?'

'No, really it was nothing. I'm tired. I want to get some sleep. I was on night duty last night.'

'Why the heck didn't you say so before? You could have snatched a few hours before taking the clinic.'

'I'm used to long hours.'

'Guy said you had been at the General. Did you like it there?' he asked as he climbed on to a wooden chair with hammer and nails ready. 'Hand me up that blanket then hold the bottom and take most of the weight.'

'It was like most hospitals,' June said doing as he had instructed.

'Did you specialize in anything?'

'No. I can do most things.'

'English nurses usually can. I've got a

64

great respect for their skill. You're not the first one I've worked with.'

'One of the nurses in my section said she knew you. Jacqueline Fraser, do you remember her?'

'Sure. Her brother and I went through UBC together.'

'Oh? I didn't know the university had a training school.'

'A real good one. It had ten faculties then, more now I guess. We took a post-graduate course in medicine. Surgery I took up later in the States.'

'What made you take this post?'

'That's too long a story and not for publication.' He hammered hard. 'Now move along! I want to nail the other side.'

When he had finished he jumped down and eyed his handiwork with satisfaction. 'That should do you tonight. No one can see through that. I chose the thickest one.'

'Thanks Doctor. I'm very grateful.'

He gave her a keen look. 'You did see something out there, didn't you?'

She bit her lips. 'Perhaps. I couldn't be certain.'

'I can,' he retorted grimly. 'We can soon fix that. I can make the Mission House out of bounds after ten o'clock.'

'Oh no! Please don't do that. It will only draw attention to me. Let everyone settle down. They will soon get used to me.'

'I can't see that happening. If there's any unpleasantness I shall send you back.'

'You would like that, wouldn't you Doctor Tretton?'

He glanced quickly at her challenging face. 'Yes!' he said vehemently. 'That would suit me down to the ground. I never wanted you here. It was Guy who insisted I have you.'

The door banged with a crash behind him. June feeling shaken and unhappy sank down on to the bed. It was going to be much worse than she had anticipated, she told herself miserably. The doctor really hated her being there. How was she going to keep her temper with such a man?

But she felt so dreadfully weary that for the moment she could not think of anything except getting her head down on to the pillow as quickly as possible.

Even Doctor Tretton can't make me leave if I don't want to go, she thought sleepily as she nestled into the warmth of the soft blankets. I can be as stubborn as he is!

CHAPTER THREE

June awoke early the next morning. Maybe it was the unfamiliar bed or perhaps the loud and vibrant chorus of birds in the trees and bushes surrounding the camp which had aroused her. Whatever it was she did not mind having to get up for she felt wonderfully rested and eager to begin the day.

She tied back the blanket Harley had nailed over the window and as she did so heard the deep voices of the men who were making their way to the canteen for first breakfast. As she intended to clean out the cupboards in the clinic she did not put on her uniform but chose a washable cotton dress which needed no ironing. She had yet to discover whether the camp possessed an iron and thought it very unlikely. Having plenty of time she did not hurry deciding to start on the linen cupboard which she had noticed was very untidy. There to her joy she discovered a roll of fine cheesecloth. It was extremely wide and there was yards of it. Enough for a flimsy curtain at my window, she thought with satisfaction. But ought I to ask Doctor Tretton first?

Resolving not to put a foot wrong on this first day she set the roll aside and continued foraging and by the time she had turned out all the cupboards she had gained a fair idea of the amount of equipment the Mission possessed. It took her nearly two hours before she had replaced the contents and by then she was feeling hungry.

She washed and changed into her uniform then walked across to the canteen. There she found it less embarrassing than the evening before because most of the men had left the camp. A few were consuming piles of flap-jacks and amongst them was Doctor Tretton. He raised his hand to her but did not signal for her to sit next to him. With faint relief she chose a seat near the door and ate toast and marmalade with several cups of coffee, not at all bothered by her solitary state.

She had nearly finished when Harley came over and sat down opposite to her. 'I have to call in at an outlying farm. It will take me most of the day. You think you can cope here?'

She nodded. 'What do you want me to do?'

'Something will turn up, I guess. I've never had a day without one mishap.' He broke off eyeing her starched cap quizzically.

'There's no need to dress yourself up like that. We haven't a hospital and it's stupid to pretend we have. It looks so ... theatrical.'

'As long as I know,' she said carelessly hiding her annoyance for he had been extremely blunt. 'What would you prefer me to wear?'

'Anything but that ridiculous outfit.'

'Very well that's easily remedied. By the water Doctor Tretton, is there an iron in camp?'

'An iron?' raising his eyebrows.

'Yes, the usual sort for pressing clothes.'

He smiled. 'I guess not. Men don't bother to iron their shirts.'

'Then it's just as well that I needn't wear my uniform. I found a roll of cheesecloth in one of the cupboards. Would you have any objections if I cut it up for curtains?'

'Sure, why not. I didn't know we had it.'

'It was pushed right to the back of the linen cupboard.'

'It's okay. You can use anything you want within reason. If you have any casualties do make a few notes. I like to know what is going on.'

'Naturally. Doctor. I will see to it.'

'That's it then. I'm off now. See you later on.'

June felt rather depressed after that. It looked as if she was going to have a boring day. But as things turned out the hours passed swiftly. She had no sooner reached the clinic than one of the men came rushing across from the canteen saying that the cook had scalded his arm and would she come right away.

Swiftly gathering up the things she might need she hurried back with him. She dressed the injured man's arm, gave him something to ease the pain and then returned to her room to change out of her uniform. Ten minutes later a man holding a wooden pole and a carpenter's bag appeared on the scene.

'Doc asked me to fix up a curtain rail for you,' he explained as he walked noisily across the hall.

She showed him into her room, watched him scatter his tools over the floor and left him to get on with it. Nearly an hour went by before he came to the clinic door where June was sterilizing the equipment.

'What about a cup of coffee, Nurse?'

She nodded thinking that it was fortunate that she had put fresh coffee in the pot before she had placed it on the stove which some unseen person kept stoked up. Deciding to have one with him she took two cups in with her and listened patiently to a boring dialogue about various ailments the man imagined he had. Assuring him that none of them was fatal she took the empty cups away and hoped that he would continue his task with more speed. To her mind he was taking rather a long time fixing that rail.

The gong sounded for the mid-day meal and wearing serviceable jeans and a long sleeved, white blouse she went across to the canteen with the carpenter in tow.

'How much longer are you going to be?' she enquired as they went into the dining hut.

'I'm nearly finished. Doc said I was to

make a good job. I couldn't find any brackets so I've been making them from pieces of wood.'

Regretting her censure of the time he had taken June spoke to him more cordially and the meal passed quickly. She asked after the cook before she left, had a quick check on his arm and went back to the clinic. The carpenter had finished and was sweeping up the shavings of wood.

'Why, that's splendid,' she said sincerely. 'You obviously know how to use those tools.'

'I sure do. That's my line. I made that table for Doc and the chair and bookcase in your room. He finds me real useful I can tell you.'

'I'm sure he does. Thanks very much. I suppose there aren't any curtain rings?'

He shook his head. 'I could make some I guess from wire.'

'Don't bother,' she replied hastily thinking that she had taken up enough of his time. 'I can make some big loops with tape and stitch them on. We have plenty of that.'

'Okay. Anytime you want anything done don't mind asking. It makes a change from felling trees.'

Eager to make her curtains June did not keep him talking and by four o'clock she had threaded tape through the hemmed cheesecloth and put the curtain up. Then she stitched circles of tape on the red blanket and threaded the pole through them. The effect of the two colours, red and white was very pleasing and she was admiring the startling difference it made to the room when Harley looked in.

'Here you are! It was so quiet I thought you had run away.' He gazed at the curtains with an amused smile on his lips. 'Real nice! That should keep the snoopers at bay.'

'Your carpenter did a good job.'

'Sure has. We will ask the bush pilot to bring in a few rings.'

'I shouldn't bother. As you said I may

not be here that long.'

'Oh?' He gave her an intent look. 'Changed your mind about staying? Have you had a boring day?'

'On the contrary. It's passed quickly. How was your patient?'

'Not too good. She's had one miscarriage and the way she's going she may have another.'

'A maternity case? That's the last thing I imagined I would be involved with here.'

'Have you taken a course on midwifery?'

'Yes. You don't have to worry about that.'

'I'm not. Anyway I doubt whether we shall have to handle it. I've told Stan he ought to send his wife to hospital a couple of months before the baby is due but she won't hear of it.'

'She wants to stay on the farm? I suppose she's working as usual?'

'That's the trouble. She ought to be resting. I can't make her see sense. She says she's scared to leave.'

'Would it help if I went to see her?'

He eyed her speculatively. 'It might. You can try. Leave it for a few days. I will ask one of the men to drive you over.'

'Couldn't I drive myself?'

'No. It's a good forty miles through dense bush with a river to cross. It's too dangerous.'

'You went on your own.'

'Sure, that's different.'

'I can't see why. You are only saying I can't go alone because I'm a woman. That shouldn't stop me doing my job. I'm willing to take the risk.'

'Is that so?' His eyes glinted. 'Well, I'm not allowing you to go alone. I make the decisions here. You can see now why I prefer a male assistant.'

June's chin was slightly defiant. 'As you haven't got one it might be more gracious to accept the fact and give me a chance to prove myself.'

'So far I haven't done or said anything!' he said reproachfully.

'You don't have to say it with words.'

He looked at her unsmilingly. 'Are you trying to pick a quarrel with me, Nurse Bentley?'

'No!' June shrugged her shoulders. 'It's very difficult to hold a conversation with you. You're so prejudiced. I don't mind hardship and I'm certain I can do my job as well as any male assistant.'

'Only time will show. For the moment I expect you to obey my orders. I hear there was an accident in the canteen?'

June smiled wryly. 'They soon told you about that! George upset a pan of boiling water over himself. He was lucky to escape with a blistered arm. I've made a note of the treatment.'

'That guy's always having accidents! Real careless he is. A few weeks ago he set himself alight.'

'How did he do that?'

'Left a utensil in the pan and the handle caught alight. Next thing he knew his overall was on fire. Luckily the man who was helping him dowsed him with water. No damage done except rather a mess in the canteen.'

'That's easy to do. I've done it myself. All handles ought to be made un-inflammable.'

'Did you catch yourself alight?'

'No. Being a coward I stepped back and let the thing burn itself out.'

'George is too stupid to think of that. He's a real menace. Any day now I expect to find the canteen in flames.'

'What do they cook with, oil?'

'Sure. It's cheaper and easier. We have it flown in.'

'That seems strange when there is so much of it here.'

'Crude oil. We need the refined stuff.'

'How do they get the oil away from here?'

'Through pipe lines. Some run right across Canada to Montreal. Didn't your fiancé tell you about it?'

'No.' She frowned then said quietly,

'I've only had one letter from him since he's been here. That's why I wanted this posting.'

'Haven't you heard from your brother either?'

'Andy hates writing letters. I've had one or two notes. I asked him why Chris hadn't written but he never answered.'

'I guess he has been too busy. This new find has given the men plenty of head-aches. That's why they fixed up a bush-camp on the spot.'

'It may be that,' she said doubtfully. 'I wish I could visit their camp.'

He stroked his chin thoughtfully. 'I might be able to do something about that. I will have a word with the crews' boss. You will have to have his permission.'

'Oh would you?' June's face brightened. 'I would be so grateful.'

'Don't be too optimistic. Joe isn't the easiest of men to ask for a favour.' He glanced at her curiously. 'Have you known Chris long?'

She laughed lightly. 'Nearly all my life. We grew up together.'

'Is that so? Maybe that's the reason you haven't heard from him.'

She looked surprised. 'I don't understand. Why do you think that?'

He shrugged his broad shoulders carelessly. 'Knowing you so well I guess he takes you for granted. You sure you're in love with the guy?'

She said stiffly. 'I'm engaged to him.'

'That doesn't answer my question.' He smiled his grey eyes slightly mocking. 'I know. It's none of my business. I will save you the trouble of telling me.'

'Thanks,' she said dryly.

'At least you have the good sense not to quarrel with me.' He was turning towards the door when he asked abruptly, 'When do you intend to marry Chris?'

'We haven't arranged a date. Chris wanted to get established first.'

'To my mind that's a mistake. If he wants to marry you he ought to get on with it. No point in hanging about.'

She smiled faintly. 'You're making it difficult for me to keep my temper, Doctor.'

'I guess so.' He grinned. 'As you may be here for a month at least you will have to get used to me. I usually say what I think. I will be off now and leave you in peace.'

June felt rather subdued after he had left. If he had but known it he had rammed home the truth with uncanny accuracy. Chris had never been an ardent lover and June had nearly despaired of ever getting him to the point of asking her to marry him. Then a short while before he was due to start his job in Smoky River he had surprised June with a proposal. I suppose he thought I might meet someone else, she mused. It was not a very happy occasion even then for he was so offhanded about it and refused to discuss when we would marry. We ought to have married long ago when we first became attracted to one another. Is he looking forward to seeing me? He must have heard that I'm here by now.

No one had attended the clinic that afternoon so there was not much she could do to keep her mind occupied. It's no good worrying, she thought. Everything will be all right when I see Chris again.

Evidently Harley lost no time in speaking to Joe for after the evening meal the foreman caught June up as she was leaving the canteen.

'Evening, Nurse,' he drawled giving her a faint smile. 'Doc has been telling me you want to visit the new rig.'

She nodded, admiring the strength of his short body and his crinkled, leathery face under a shock of coarse grey hair. He was older than the other men and far more experienced judging by the quiet air of authority with which he spoke.

'My brother and my fiancé are working there,' she explained. 'I would be grateful if you would allow me to see them.'

'I don't much care for having you out there,' he said bluntly. 'We are working flat out to get the derrick up. We have to know how much oil is there before we can ask for more men. Don't look so disappointed! I tell you what I will do. They can both come back here for a spell. The break might do them good.'

June smiled and took his hand impetuously. 'That would be marvellous! Thanks so much Mr Skinner!'

He was amused by her excitement. 'That's okay, Nurse. Only too pleased to oblige.' He turned to retrace his steps and seeing Harley strolling towards them raised his hand in recognition.

June was still standing where Joe had left her and started when Harley spoke to her.

'Such a starry expression means I was successful, I guess,' he drawled a half tender smile curving his lips. 'There's no need to look so elated. Remember the higher one goes the farther it is to fall.'

She laughed. 'It means a lot to me.'

'So I see,' he said dryly. 'I reckon I might have been wrong about Chris Ferris.'

She smiled slightly astonished that he admitted he might have erred then after a few minutes left him to return to the Mission House. She had not been inside long before she was startled by the screech of brakes as a truck pulled up outside. Rushing to the door she met the driver who was looking very agitated.

'Is Doc here?' he asked quickly.

'No. I think he's gone to his cabin. Can I help?'

'I've brought in an injured man. He got caught by a falling tree. He's real bad. I think Doc ought to see him.'

'Send someone across for the Doctor,' June said as she ran down the steps. 'No don't bother! He's coming over here.'

Harley had heard the truck drive at terrific speed across the clearing and had guessed that there had been an accident.

He had begun to run and had nearly reached the Mission when June saw him. After a few tense questions to the driver Harley climbed into the truck.

'Would you get a stretcher?' June asked the driver. 'There's one in the waiting-room.'

After he had gone she hurriedly pulled a bed out from the side wall then dashed into the clinic to collect clean linen and blankets. Luckily she had put a kettle of water on the stove to heat some time before and it was nearly boiling. She pushed it to the middle of the stove then quickly made up the bed. She was just finishing when the doctor and the driver came in with the injured man on the stretcher. Glancing at him anxiously she saw that he was only a youngster of nineteen or so.

Harley was looking grim. 'Fetch my bag from the surgery, Nurse!' he said curtly. 'I'm going to scrub up.'

June hurried to do as she was bid,

noticed an unbroken packet of gauze on a shelf and took that also. The driver stood back and watched them nervously. June filled a hypodermic needle and gave the injured boy an injection and after a few seconds he ceased to groan. Harley hacked the jacket away from the boy's crushed body with a knife dropping the pieces on the floor in his haste. June wiped the blood from the injured man's face noticing with alarm that it was returning swiftly as it oozed from his mouth and nose.

'Internal injuries,' Harley said tersely. 'Find Joe and ask him to send a radio message. This lad will have to be flown out tonight.'

'Sure. If Joe's not around I will send it myself.' The driver turned and ran out banging the door after him.

'Why the heck do they allow these youngsters to come up here!' Harley said angrily, his grey cycs steely as he looked at June. 'I can't do much except patch him up. He needs X-rays, surgery and specialized treatment. Get the oxygen out, Nurse. I guess that's about all we can do, just keep him alive.'

The young man breathed more easily after that and June set about dressing the superficial wounds for he was covered in cuts and bruises.

'Do you want me to fly back with him?' she asked as she bathed the lad's hands.

'No. Good of you to offer but they will have a doctor on the plane. Guy has all that organized.' Harley smiled twistedly. 'He's good at putting the cart before the horse. If only he would listen to me we wouldn't have to deal with these terrible accidents.'

'He does look young,' June remarked.

'Oh, it's not his age. Some lads are capable of doing a man's job. This one knows little of bush layout. Look at his hands! They are as smooth as yours. Another greenhorn Guy has sent up without sufficient training!'

'Where will they take him?'

'Grande Prairie. Guy keeps a plane there for emergencies. It won't take long. The lad will be in hospital within an hour.'

June tucked the blanket in tightly. They had not lifted the boy from the stretcher but rested it on top of the bed.

'Time to go, Nurse,' Harley said flicking a glance at his watch. 'Find that driver and tell him we are taking the lad to the air-field. We don't want to waste precious minutes. The plane ought to arrive shortly.'

In the darkness as they waited for the plane to come in, June had a few minutes to reflect on the work she was doing. After tonight she would no longer believe that she was wasting her energies with minor accidents. At the moment it seemed more worthwhile than being one of many in a well-run hospital. She also understood a little better why Harley stayed. He was the vital link between patient and hospital. And much depended on his instant decision.

She had remained in the truck with the

patient but because of the flares she could see Harley's tall figure silhouetted against the trees. He was talking to the driver whom June had discovered was the injured boy's cousin. The lad had only been in the camp a couple of weeks. Bitten with excitement for adventure he had skipped his last year at high school and had signed on to work as a logger. June could understand Harley's anger. With boys like that it was inevitable that some of them would come to grievous harm. She wished that she could do something but could not see how she could help.

When the plane had flown off with the injured boy plus brief notes from Harley, the driver of the truck drove off and left June and Harley to find their own way back to the camp. In the star-studded sky a wisp of a moon floated high above the dark tree tops. June shivered, suddenly conscious of how chilled she had become for she had not stopped to put on a coat.

'It's not so far,' Harley said taking her hand and tucking it into the pocket of his jacket with his own warm fingers. 'Keep close to me and you will soon feel better.'

'Couldn't the driver have taken us back?'

'I told him to go on. He was anxious to return the truck. He borrowed it from a transport company who are loading logs.'

'Has he far to go?'

'A good few miles. The company is felling trees on a new site. The transport firm are sub-contractors. They have their own camp which they allow the company to use. If the oil find is worthwhile then a settlement will spring up joining the camp with that one.'

'Does Guy control all these sites?'

'He does, worse luck. He may be a good executive but to my mind he takes too many chances with human life. To give him his due he sees that the man are comfortable. They have to be housed and fed. Our camp holds about fifty men. But that's not many once the operation is in full swing. He's getting ready to ship in another fifty.'

'One doctor and a nurse won't be enough then,' June said. The warmth from Harley's body was beginning to steal through to her and she felt less cold than she had been.

'They will have to build a hospital then. Guy won't like it. He's tight with money.'

'Will you run it?'

'I hadn't considered it. But now you mention it, I guess not. I tangle with Guy too much and lose my temper. The number of accidents we have make me see red. He sends too many kids up here.'

'Why does he do it?'

'Cheap labour, I guess. He relies on the skilled men to carry the untrained. It's false economy. Sometimes I wonder if the Senior Partner knows what is going on.'

'Couldn't you do something? If you sent in a report that might attract attention.'

'I've done that and nothing happened. I shall have to think of something else.'

The camp was quiet and in darkness as they crossed the clearing. Harley did not go in to the Mission with June for they had lit the lamps before they left.

He was turning to go when June said impetuously, 'I do understand why you get annoyed with Guy. He doesn't come in contact with the injured men. You have all the unpleasantness and anxiety. I do wish I could help in some way, Harley.'

He stared down at her a smile playing about his lips. 'You already have. You are the first person who has listened to me and understood.'

His eyes held hers in a steadfast gaze then suddenly he drew her towards him and before she could resist, kissed her determinedly on the mouth. His hands fell away from her almost immediately.

'Just saying, thank you,' he muttered. 'Goodnight, June.' And turning abruptly he left her, disappearing into the darkness swiftly.

June pressed the back of her hand against her lips her mind dazed with surprise and something else which she could not define. But she was conscious of a sense of elation as she went up the steps and entered the Mission House. Not once had Harley rebuked her or made sarcastic remarks yet he could have done with a male assistant that evening. She had not been strong enough to lift the injured boy. I do hope his injuries aren't too serious, she mused. I wonder how Harley would have coped if he had had to operate? Superbly I expect, she told herself sleepily. He seems to do everything well.

Two days later Andy arrived on a truck coming in for supplies. June was outside the canteen chatting to the Doctor but as soon as she saw her brother she ran across to the truck.

'Andy!' she cried. 'How marvellous to see you.'

His enfolding arms lifted her off the ground as he hugged her. There was no mistaking that they were related for Andrew's hair was almost the same colour as June's. But he was not as attractive as his sister. His hair lacked the sheen of gold which drew attention to June and his face was covered in freckles. But he had vivid blue eyes and a mouth which smiled easily.

'Did I give you a shock?' June asked with a laugh.

'You certainly did! What made you come? It can't be very comfortable. I thought you were enjoying the General?'

'It's not too bad here.' She glanced over her shoulder and noted that Harley was watching them. 'Isn't Chris with you? Joe said he could come in with you.'

'No.' Andy hesitated flicking an anxious glance at her. 'He may come in next week.'

Some of the brightness left June's face. 'Didn't he want to see me?'

95

Andy seemed uneasy as he took her arm and began to walk away from the truck. 'To tell the truth, Sis, he didn't seem very keen. He's recently been put in charge of a crew and he's taking the promotion very seriously.'

June smiled wryly. 'He finds it more important than me?'

'For the moment, yes.'

She said slowly, 'You are a crew boss, aren't you? It didn't stop you from coming to see me.'

'Perhaps it was easier for me.' Andy appeared reluctant to continue and his voice became deeper. 'You will find out eventually so I might as well tell you. Since we've been at Smoky River, Chris and I haven't exactly hit it off. He resented me being over him and he's done his best to make me feel uncomfortable.' His mouth tightened grimly as he finished.

'But why?' June asked her blue eyes dismayed. 'You were such good friends.'

Andy laughed shortly, 'We had never

worked together before. That's a crucial test. I've discovered to my cost that Chris is not what I supposed him to be.' He broke off looking at her apologetically. 'I'm sorry, Sis, but that's how it is.'

'I'm glad you told me. But I can't see why Chris didn't take the opportunity to come in to see me. I haven't quarrelled with him. A misunderstanding with you ought not to have kept him away.' She hesitated then asked curiously, 'Is that why he hasn't written to me?'

'I suppose so. When you asked me about him I didn't know what to say. He never mentions you.'

'Is that because he's lost interest?'

'It looks like it. Don't take it to heart, June. I had to tell you. Please don't be so upset. He never was good enough for you.'

'I've known him a long time. It's difficult to understand. When we parted he was keen enough. If he hadn't been why did he want to marry me?'

'I wouldn't count on it now.'

June bit her lips hard willing herself to appear calm. Then with an effort she said miserably, 'Didn't he send me any message?'

Andy shook his head. 'I asked him if he was going to come in with me. It wasn't easy I can tell you for we haven't spoken two words between us for days. Chris said, no, very emphatically then muttered something about parting doesn't always make the heart grow fonder. I became angry and asked him what he meant. Was he going to split up with you? He said it had already taken place. He had changed his mind. He wasn't ready to tie himself down and he thought that you were too much like me.'

'Oh!' June's face had whitened and anger made her voice shake. 'If he feels like that he might have had the decency to tell me before discussing it with you.'

'That's what I thought. Perhaps it's for the best, June. He has changed. There's no two questions about it. He intends to break with both of us. And if it wasn't for you I couldn't care less.'

June sighed. 'To think I gave up everything to emigrate with you both. Chris and I were to start a new life together or so he said before he came up here.'

Andy put his hand on her shoulder and pressed it. 'Hold on, June. So far you've taken it very well. Don't break down now. There's a chap in a white jacket looking at us.'

'I know. That's Doctor Tretton.' She swallowed the hard lump in her throat and pulled herself together. 'Shall I introduce you?'

'Not now. I haven't had a bite to eat all day. Do you think the canteen is open?'

'I'm sure they will find something for you. Go in and ask. They are very obliging. I'm going back to the Mission House. Come over after you have had your snack.'

June was sitting at the desk in the

waiting-room staring blankly ahead when Harley walked in. She did not answer him when he first spoke to her and he moved swiftly across to her.

'Something wrong, June? You look so white. What's happened? Didn't Chris Ferris come in with your brother?'

She clasped her hands tightly together in her lap. 'He was too busy,' she said stiffly.

Harley laughed. 'I can't believe that! I thought he was the reason you came up here.'

'It was.'

He stared at her perplexedly. 'Then why didn't he come?'

She caught in her breath then said sharply. 'Do you have to go on and on! Chris didn't come! That's all I can tell you.'

'Say now, there's no need to hit out at me because you're mad with your fiancé.'

'He's not my fiancé and I'm not mad,' she said, her blue eyes scarcely concealing the tears which threatened to unmask her.

A look of surprise flashed across Harley's face. He stared at her uncertainly then swiftly moved to her side. He did not touch her but she could sense the sympathy which emanated from him. Somehow his proximity was comforting, especially as he could no longer see her face.

'It's as bad as that, eh?' he said softly. 'I'm sorry. I wouldn't have shot all those questions at you if I had known.'

She put her hand to her eyes afraid that she was going to disgrace herself with tears but managed to force them back.

'Have a good weep. It will release the tension. Do you want my handkerchief?'

'No thanks,' she sniffed. 'I feel too upset to cry.'

'I know. It hurts. Do you want to talk about it?'

She smiled wryly. 'There's not much to tell. The engagement is off, that's all.'

'It's mighty sudden. Did he send Andy in to tell you?'

'Yes. It gave me a shock.'

'I bet.' Harley looked grim. 'It doesn't say much for him.'

'I suppose he didn't want to hurt me.'

'He didn't want to see you being hurt. It's a cruel and cowardly way of breaking off an engagement.' Harley looked down at her thoughtfully. 'Would you like to go back to the General?'

She shook her head. 'I'm not letting him drive me away!'

'Good, that's the spirit!' Harley said emphatically.

She glanced up lifting her dark lashes which were glistening with a suspicion of tears. 'You sound pleased! I thought you didn't want me here.'

'A man can change, can't he? Anyway that's got nothing to do with it. I don't want you defeated by one disappointment.'

She smiled faintly. 'That's just how I do feel, defeated! My entire future has been washed away. I've lost my incentive.'

'That's the first phase. Once the shock

has gone you will feel able to cope.'

She glanced up at him in surprise. 'You understand so well. It's almost as if ...' She broke off unable to continue beneath his fierce gaze.

'I've experienced it also? Sure. It's happened to me.' His mouth set grimly.

'Is that why you buried yourself in Smoky River?'

'At first, maybe. I've got over it now. I enjoy camp life.' He glanced at her thoughtfully. 'You sure your brother got it right? It seems a little difficult to believe.'

'Yes,' she said flatly. 'Andy wouldn't have said what he did if he hadn't been sure.'

Harley frowned. 'To me it seems crazy. I didn't want you to suffer unnecessarily. You might have been mistaken.'

'The fact that he didn't come in to see me ought to settle your doubts. Joe had given him permission. Chris will have to have a very exceptional excuse for that.'

'Women are such changeable creatures and some will forgive a man anything. If Chris does explain with conviction you will be back in his arms in a jiffy.'

'Perhaps.' She smiled. 'It makes no difference to you, does it? I'm not likely to marry yet. And I thought I was settling in rather well.'

'Sure, everything's dandy,' he drawled, his voice faintly sardonic. 'Isn't it time we concentrated on our work?'

'Yes. I noticed a couple of men waiting outside,' she said quickly. 'If you are busy perhaps I could deal with them.'

He smiled. 'I bet one of them is suffering from chronic indigestion. I've noticed him in the canteen. The way some of these guys shovel down their food you'd imagine they've forgotten they have teeth.'

June chuckled. 'Yes, I've noticed it also. Eating fast soon becomes a habit.'

'I had news from Grande Prairie today,' Harley remarked. 'That youngster we sent to them is doing fine.'

'That is good news! I was worried about him. I do hope we don't have any more as serious as that.'

'I shouldn't bank on it. If Guy continues to send unskilled men to Smoky River we shall have more.' He flicked an enquiring glance at her. 'Do you have any influence with him?'

June looked startled. 'No, why should I?'

'He gave you this post. It was just a thought, forget it!'

'That's impossible now you've said it. Whatever made you think I might be able to influence Guy?'

Harley stared at her frowning slightly. 'He never does anything for nothing. You are the first young woman to be sent here. It just crossed my mind that he owed you something.'

'I asked to come.'

'That wouldn't be enough.'

June's cheeks became tinged with a delicate pink colour as she guessed what he was insinuating. 'Ask Guy why he sent me!' she said sharply. 'I've only met the man twice.'

'Okay, don't get so riled! Guy never listens to me. I only wondered how friendly you were.'

'It's unlikely that we shall ever be that. I don't even like him,' she replied shortly.

'Okay, calm down! I'm beginning to wish I had never mentioned it.'

'It's a great pity you did. But it's shown me one thing very clearly, Doctor Tretton. You can't have a very high opinion of me!'

Harley gave her a cool glance then walked swiftly to the door and opened it. After the men came in for treatment there was little time for conversation. June looked calm enough but it was only natural that she was feeling indignant and after her anger abated she was conscious of a deep, overwhelming disappointment.

CHAPTER FOUR

Three days passed uneventfully. June was avoiding Harley whenever possible for there had developed a coolness between them which she found uncomfortable. His remarks about Guy and herself still rankled and she knew it would take more than a few days to forget them. He had given her the impression that he was disappointed because she had not been close enough with Guy to ask him to do something about sending untrained men to Smoky River. She had gleaned during her short stay that the matter was uppermost in Harley's mind and that it was of the utmost urgency that he do something about it. However she thought it a little unfair that he should behave as if she had refused to co-operate. If she remembered rightly she had said she would like to help.

Chris had not come in to see her and this aggravated her also. She found it difficult to believe that he had ceased to care after all they had meant to each other. Even if he had a change of heart he ought to have told her so himself. The tranquil atmosphere at the camp and the inactivity during the last few days were beginning to make her feel restless and swallowing her pride she went into Harley's surgery after the last patient had gone.

He glanced up at her unsmilingly. 'Something the matter, Nurse?' he asked curtly.

'No, nothing,' she replied quietly then said quickly, 'Could I visit Mrs Rowley tomorrow? I haven't much to do here.'

'Sure, if you want to. I will ask one of the men to drive you over.'

'It's Bill's day off tomorrow. He has offered to take me.'

'Bill? That's the Englishman, isn't it?'

He frowned. 'Okay, if you want him to take you. I may need the jeep but I will arrange with Joe for you to use a small truck.' He broke off to give her an intent look. 'It's mighty fine country west of here. Go early and make a day of it. It will do you good. You haven't been looking too well lately.'

'I feel all right,' she said defensively.

'It's natural I guess to resent sympathy but feeling sorry for yourself won't help. You've got to snap out of it.'

'I'm not sorry for myself,' she said sharply. 'I was annoyed with you because you wanted to know about Guy and me.'

'Good grief is that all! You are sensitive. If it's any comfort I didn't think there was anything between you. But I had to ask.'

'You were hoping that I could make Guy listen to me.'

He frowned. 'You've got it all wrong. You are an attractive girl. Darn it! Whatever I say you're going to think the worst. It was a chance I couldn't afford to pass. I know Guy. He would listen to a girl like you and turn a deaf ear to me.' He smiled. 'That doesn't mean I want you to get in with Guy. Far from it! I have too high a regard for you.'

June was conscious of a warmth which swiftly obliterated the strained feeling between them. She said generously, 'I'm sorry, Doctor. I wasn't at my best that day. I ought not to have taken offence.'

'I guess we were both at fault. I could have been more tactful. Have you heard from Chris Ferris?'

'No. I can't understand it. I did think he would come in to see me.'

He looked at her thoughtfully. 'Don't worry. It may be a misunderstanding. Enjoy yourself tomorrow and forget your problems. It's too bad that we have to have a slack period right now but that's how it goes. We either have nothing to do or too much.'

June left in a lighter frame of mind. In spite of Harley's bluntness and his habit of jarring raw nerves she did like him and it had worried her when they had become bad friends. But evidently he had not noticed the friction thinking that her coolness was due to her broken engagement.

She smiled to herself as she went in search of Bill. Harley's good for me, she thought. He has a knack of putting me in my place which is just as well, perhaps. My problems aren't that important. A male assistant wouldn't have behaved so erratically. What's got into me? I never used to become resentful and I would never have dreamed of showing my unhappiness to anyone at the General. It was a little different of course. I did have free time to pull myself together. That's the trouble here. I'm never off duty. I have to be ready for emergencies at any time.

Driving away from the camp early the next morning June was conscious of a sense of excitement almost as if something wonderful was going to happen. The pines smelt sweet in the fresh morning air. It was good to be able to drive through the forests of the rugged land and revel in the beauties which slowly unfolded as they penetrated the lonely, seldom used lanes. She noticed that Bill looked more relaxed and happy and guessed that he was looking forward to a day away from the camp.

The road was unmade, a rutted track cut through the bush by a succession of heavy vehicles. June was surprised at the density of the undergrowth and the closeness of the tall trees which almost blotted out the blue sky. So it was a delightful change when they emerged into a long shallow valley possessing a small silver lake.

'One of the few near here,' Bill explained. 'Although you couldn't see it we have been following the Smoky River. It empties some of its flow into the lake before branching off again. Beautiful isn't it with that backdrop of dark hills?'

Then they were skirting those wooded hills where ferns almost eight feet high covered the bottom slopes, their light greenery contrasting superbly with the blackness of the trees higher up. After twenty miles June understood why Harley had insisted that she have someone with her. Frequently they had to climb down from the truck to remove fallen trees or rocks from the track.

'Are there any dangerous animals in the forests?' she asked after one such incident.

'I've never seen any. In winter maybe. Cougars come down from the hills to find food. I've heard men talk about them. Quite a bit of hunting goes on around here; for deer mostly and there's fishing and duck shooting. Trouble is it's so easy to get lost. Most hunters bring a guide with them.'

They reached the Rowley homestead around eleven o'clock. It had no fences or gates and Bill had to drive slowly to avoid running over the geese and chickens which appeared to be everywhere. They stopped at the foot of a grass verge in front of the wooden house. A woman and a young girl were standing on the porch looking at them curiously.

'I'm Nurse Bentley,' June called out after she had climbed down from the truck. 'This is Bill one of the oil-men from Smoky River camp. Doctor Tretton asked me to call in.'

'Come right in, Nurse!' The dark-haired woman said hospitably. 'I'm Agnes Rowley. This is my niece, Emily. She's staying with us for awhile.'

She opened the screen door and waited for June and Bill to go inside then let it slam behind Emily and herself. 'Go straight through to the kitchen. I guess you're ready for a cup of coffee.'

Within a few minutes the coffee had been poured out and a plate had been piled high with cookies. Sitting at the table June had a good chance to study the two women. The excitement of their arrival had sent the colour to Agnes' cheeks but it only served to accentuate her normal pallor. She ought to have looked far healthier and fatter. She's much too thin, June thought and there's too much tension in her manner. Emily had given her a slight jolt at first for she had not expected to see such a pretty girl. Her hair was long and golden with deep waves close to her small head. With her pointed face and huge dark brown eyes she attracted ones' attention immediately. But the girl did not look very happy and June felt a little curious about her.

'You gave me quite a surprise, Nurse,' Agnes said with a smile. 'Doctor Tretton never mentioned you. I'm real glad he's got around to having a woman help him. It will make such a difference. Isn't that so, Emily?'

The girl nodded and looked at Bill who was eating the cookies one after the other. 'I made those,' she remarked proudly. 'Would you like to take some back with you?'

'Emily takes her cooking too seriously,' Agnes said quickly before Bill could answer. 'She comes from Grande Prairie. She's eighteen and just finished high school. As she couldn't make up her mind what she wanted to do Stan suggested that she come and stay with us. He thought I ought to have someone with me.'

'That's what I've come to talk to you about.' June glanced at Bill. 'Would you mind leaving us alone? Perhaps Emily would show you round the farm?'

'Sure.' Bill got to his feet. 'Call out when you have finished.'

'It won't take long.' She waited until Emily and Bill had gone then said pleasantly, 'Can I wash my hands, Mrs Rowley? I ought to examine you; just to see if all's well. Have you a bedroom we could use?'

When they returned to the kitchen June said quietly, 'The doctor is right, Agnes. You ought to be in hospital. It's not going to be an easy birth.'

'I didn't expect it to be,' the woman said sharply. 'I'm in good health, better than last time.'

'You will have to be very careful. No heavy work at all. Believe me you could so easily lose the child after too much exertion. You need to rest more and more as the time draws nearer. If you went to hospital you wouldn't have to do anything.'

'I know that but I can't leave Stan. It's a lonely life. Except for a few stray visitors we never see anyone.'

'It depends on how much you want this child,' June said cautiously. 'It would only mean three months. What's that in a lifetime? Isn't your husband willing to sacrifice his comfort for a few weeks? Doesn't he want to be a father?'

Agnes looked indignant. 'I didn't say it was Stan who was stopping me from going. He was real disappointed the last time. I couldn't face letting him down again.'

'If you feel so strongly about it why

don't you agree to go to hospital?' June said in some surprise. 'Is there a financial difficulty? Forgive me but I have to ask.'

'No. The homestead is doing well enough. We can afford it. I would go if I was certain I was going to have the baby.'

'Doctor Tretton said you were rather frightened about going.' June smiled. 'You don't strike me as that kind of woman. Why if you were timid you wouldn't be living so far north. I've been here long enough to see that the life is hard on women.'

'I'm not scared of the birth! You don't understand. It's going all that way. I would feel such a failure.'

'I'm beginning to see what you are getting at. If you had a miscarriage here it wouldn't seem to be your fault. The odds would be against you. But if it happened in hospital with everything in your favour then you would blame yourself. That's it isn't it?'

'Yes,' Agnes said despondently. 'I keep thinking of when I come back here and explain to Stan.'

June said gently, 'I do sympathize, Agnes. I would feel the same. Any woman would. But there is another side to it. Wouldn't you feel worse if you stayed on and lost the baby? Wouldn't you blame yourself because you hadn't done the best thing to ensure the baby's safety? Wouldn't you imagine that you hadn't given the child a chance? Supposing you had a two year old child now and it became ill. Would you refuse to take him to hospital? Would you insist that the child remain here? You know you wouldn't. You would do anything to help him get better.'

Agnes was looking bewildered. 'I think I can see what you are getting at. I hadn't thought of it like that before. I've been real selfish only thinking of my own feelings not considering the life of the child. He has the right to be considered first.'

'I believe that. But you must make

the decision, Agnes. I can only give you advice.'

The woman was silent for a few moments then she nodded. 'You have made it so clear. There's no two doubts about it. I shall have to go. How stupid of me not to have thought of it myself! Stan and I don't matter. We ought to have realized that when we decided to have a child.'

June smiled. 'I'm so pleased, Agnes. I will tell the doctor that you have agreed to go. He will make all the arrangements, I'm sure. There will be nothing to worry about. You will be in good hands. And whatever the outcome you will know that you did all you could.' She paused, then to take the woman's mind off the recent conversation, said, 'Tell me about your niece. She's a pretty girl. What does she want to do?'

'Yes, she always was pretty even as a child. Her mother, my sister has fair hair too and big brown eyes. The girl is at an awkward age. I'm worried about her. She's been real restless ever since she came. She needs more company than I can give her. After Doctor Tretton paid us a couple of visits she mooned about the place like a sick cow. It was plain to see that she fell real hard for him. Only a girlish crush, you know, but real irritating I can tell you. I did wonder at first if it would develop into something serious for the doctor was taken with her. I could see that. It seems such a shame that they can't see more of each other. It doesn't give them a chance being so far away. Didn't the doctor mention Emily to you, Nurse?'

'No I was surprised to see her.'

'That's a good sign, I reckon. He can't bring himself to talk about her. What's the accommodation like at the camp? Would there be room for Emily to stay for a while?'

June swiftly hid her astonishment. 'I don't really know. If it was an emergency I suppose we could fit her in.'

'Couldn't you make it an emergency?'

Agnes' brown eyes were eager.

June found the idea of playing cupid to Doctor Tretton and Emily highly amusing if not slightly ludicrous. But supposing the woman was right? Harley could be attracted to the girl. She *was* lovely. And it would be frustrating to have her so many miles away for he couldn't leave the camp too often. Something might happen whilst he was away. I could pretend that I wanted Emily to stay, she thought undecidedly. There would be no harm in that, surely? Yes, it would be natural for me to want another girl around.

'It will be all right, Agnes,' she said smilingly. 'Emily can come back with me. We will fit her in somewhere.'

Agnes sighed with relief. 'That's mighty nice of you, Nurse. If you go and tell Emily I will start getting her things together.'

With a frightening sense that she had done something she was going to regret later, June walked through the house and out on to the porch. She hesitated there eyeing the sweep of short grass where some cattle grazed then turned her gaze on the untidy group of sheds close to a ploughed field. As she walked away from the house she could hear pigs grunting and eventually came to a wide trough where they were feeding. Chickens pecked the ground annoying the piglets who were fighting to get to their mothers. June shooed the chickens away and uttering protesting squawks they flew off into the bush. She thought that it was the most disordered farm she had seen yet but as Agnes had said they were doing well, June supposed that neither of the Rowleys bothered about the look of the place.

Seeing no sign of Bill or Emily she turned her back on the squealing pigs and hearing a truck driving at speed, hurried back to the open ground. The sun felt warm on her hair and shoulders for she had discarded her jacket and wore only her jeans and a white blouse. The truck was making for the house but when the driver saw her he pulled up beside her.

June recognized the man and was too astonished to say much.

'Chris!' she exclaimed.

'Hello, June,' he said flatly, his hazel eyes uneasily scanning her delighted face. 'Pleased to see me?'

'What a stupid question!' She smiled taking in his stocky figure, rather tense square face and mop of light brown hair.

'You look nice,' he said awkwardly, moving as if to kiss her then changing his mind.

June carefully hid her disappointment at his lack of enthusiasm. 'I was expecting to see you before this. Why didn't you come with Andy?'

He shrugged his wide shoulders. 'It was difficult. I had my job to think of and your brother made me mad. What did he tell you?'

She glanced at him uncertainly. 'He said that you and he had quarrelled. Naturally I was upset that you didn't come. After all

124

we are or were engaged.'

'I know you were troubled. Doctor Tretton told me.'

June looked surprised. 'You've seen the doctor? So that's how you knew I was here!'

'Yes. He suggested I come and see you. He spoke to Joe and arranged for me to have leave.'

'Now you are annoyed that you were more or less forced to come?'

'No! I was glad of the opportunity of seeing you without Andy knowing.'

She shook her head. 'Andy doesn't mind. He's as upset as I am that things have gone wrong between you.'

'I haven't come to talk about Andy,' he said curtly. 'Why did you come to Smoky River?'

She smiled. 'Surely you know the answer to that. I came to see you. You hadn't answered my letters. I was worried about you.' She broke off to stare at him doubtfully. 'Chris, what's wrong? If you want to end our engagement, please say so and get it over with.'

'It's not like that. I don't want to give you up. But I don't want you to get ideas about marrying soon.'

She laughed. 'I wasn't expecting to settle down right away. I refused an engagement ring if you remember? We have to save some money first.'

'Shall we move away from here?' Chris said casting a glance over his shoulder at the house. 'I can't stay long. I have to get back.'

'Have you far to go?'

'No. Our camp is only twenty miles west of here. But I like to keep an eye on my men. I'm a crew boss now and that means added responsibility.'

'So I heard. Your work is important to you isn't it?'

'Naturally,' he said rather stiffly as if she had asked a silly question. 'Joe is pleased and I'm hoping for more promotion. So you can see I haven't time for distractions.'

'Meaning me?' June asked, amused by his pompous tone of voice. And she was surprised when he replied very seriously:

'Yes. I wish you hadn't come. You said you were happy working at the General. Why didn't you stay there? You would have heard soon enough if anything had happened to me.'

June's eyes lost their brightness. 'I was lonely there and worried. You have changed, Chris. I thought you would want to see me.'

He said irritably, 'What's the point if it's only for a few minutes! You must see I can't dance attendance on you. There aren't any women in the camps. How are my men going to react if they know my girl is not far away.'

'Envious, I imagine.'

'That's right! I can't afford to take the chance of any friction. I need their respect. So far they can see that I'm a hundred per cent involved in the job. And that's how it's got to be.'

'I see.' June looked at him as if she was seeing him for the first time clearly. 'You want me to return to the General?'

'I knew you would see sense.' He put his arm about her waist and drew her towards him. 'I do intend to marry you.'

June escaped from the kiss she sensed was coming and moved away to a safe distance. 'When you are ready,' she said flatly.

'Yes. You do understand don't you?'

'Perfectly.'

She was casting around for a few words which would tactfully end the conversation about their marriage when Bill and Emily ran out from the bush and almost bumped into them. June introduced them to Chris but she could sense that he was not interested and suggested that they walk up to the house.

Chris pulled June away from the other two and said quickly, 'I'm leaving now. I hope you will think over what I've said. If you decide to go back let me know and I will come in to see you before you depart.'

'I hardly think that will be necessary,' she said dryly. 'I think we've said all that we need to say.'

He nodded. 'You stay with your friends. I've enjoyed our meeting, June.'

She knew that he would not attempt to embrace her because Emily and Bill were watching and was conscious of relief. She was not at all sure how she felt; flattened perhaps, hurt and a little angry. Why on earth didn't he break it off when I gave him the chance, she asked herself in bewilderment. He's not in love with me. He's scared of cutting the threads. He wants to cling on secure in the knowledge that I will wait until he's sorted it all out. It's incredible! How could he have changed so quickly? She smiled ruefully. Perhaps it is I who has altered not Chris, she thought. I'm just seeing him as he really is. What an unsatisfactory arrangement!

'June!' Bill was staring at her curiously.

'Did we interrupt something? Your friend left rather abruptly.'

'He has to get back.' She glanced at him in surprise. 'I thought you knew Chris Ferris.'

'I've seen him around. I didn't know he was connected with you.'

'He's not,' she said carelessly. 'He used to be friendly with my brother.'

Bill looked uncertainly at her tight face then said quietly, 'We ought to be getting back to the house. Emily says her aunt is expecting us to stay for a meal.'

'That's right,' the girl drawled. 'I went back a few minutes ago and the table is set. She sent me to fetch you.'

June glanced at her fob watch. It was well after two o'clock. The time had gone quickly! 'I'm sorry Bill. You must be hungry. But we can't be too long.'

'That's okay.' He smiled at Emily who was walking beside him. 'I filled up on cookies.'

Agnes had set out quite a spread. She

had opened cans of meat, fruit and jars of home-made pickles. With creamed potatoes to eat with the meat and thick cream from the farm to decorate the fruit it soon became a delicious meal.

'You ought not to have gone to all that trouble,' June said after they had finished. 'A sandwich would have done.'

Agnes chuckled. 'Bill might not have thought so. I don't often have visitors. I would have been real disappointed if you hadn't stayed.'

Insisting that Agnes should rest June washed the dishes with Emily and Bill assisting. It took some time for the water had to be heated on the wood stove.

'Real old fashioned, isn't it?' Emily remarked as she watched June put the dishes into the shallow sink. 'Mom complains every time she visits her sister but Aunt only laughs. She says she's used to it.'

'I expect all the money goes back into the homestead,' June said. 'It can't be easy for small land owners nowadays.'

'It sure is hard. There aren't many left. Uncle has been on the land all his life. He's real proud of this place.'

By the time they had finished it was four o'clock and Agnes was up, looking fresh and eager to make tea for them.

'We don't usually have it. Supper's our next meal but I know you English folk like a cup about now.'

'We ought to be getting back,' June said regretfully. Agnes had said nothing to her niece about going with them and she was hoping that she had changed her mind.

'It won't take long. The water is boiling. I haven't told Emily the good news yet. I didn't mention it before because I know how excited she gets.'

'What news? What are you talking about, Aunt?' Emily glanced at Agnes and then at June. 'You both look mysterious.'

June laughed uneasily. 'Your aunt wants you to come back to Smoky River camp and stay with us.'

The girl looked astonished. 'Whatever for? Don't you need me here, Aunt Agnes?'

'I've been real glad of your company, Emily but I've decided to go to Grande Prairie fairly soon. I know you are bored with the life here. I thought a change might help. Wouldn't you like to stay with Nurse at the camp?'

'I guess so.' Emily looked at her uncertainly. 'I was told to keep an eye on you.'

'I don't need anyone!' Her aunt said sharply. 'Stan is real considerate. He won't allow me to do too much.'

June was beginning to suspect that Emily's welfare was not the main reason for Agnes' request. It looked very much as if the girl was getting on the woman's nerves and she was taking the opportunity to get rid of her.

'If you don't want to stay in camp with us you could take the next plane back to Grande Prairie,' June said carefully.

'No! I can't go back.' Emily flicked a

resentful glance at her aunt. 'Okay, if I'm not wanted here I might as well come with you. I reckon I shall have to pack my belongings.'

'No need,' Agnes said quickly. 'I've packed for you. Tell your Ma I'm coming to see her.'

Emily glanced at her reproachfully. 'You know I can't go home.'

'Never mind dear. I will write and tell her. Now do have a good time and enjoy yourself.'

Feeling sorry for the girl who was looking dazed and unhappy, June said quickly, 'We really have to go. It's nearly six o'clock. It will be dark before we reach the camp.'

'Couldn't you stay and meet Stan? He will be in soon and I'm sure he will want to have a talk with you, Nurse.' Agnes asked.

June shook her head. 'Doctor Tretton will call in and see you. Your husband can arrange things with him. I'm sorry, Mrs Rowley but we do have to leave now.'

Bill went down to the truck taking Emily's case with him and June quickly followed him. It seemed ages before Emily finally ran from the house. She looked as if she had been weeping and June wondered about the relationship between the two women. Evidently it had not been a very happy one judging by the pallor and tears on Emily's young face.

June said kindly, 'There's room in front, Emily. Sit between Bill and me then we won't disturb you when we have to get down to clear the road.'

'How long did it take you to get here?' Emily asked making an effort to speak naturally.

'Over three hours, I think. Oh dear! We are going to be late.'

'There's no need to worry,' Bill said cheerfully. 'Doc knows what the roads are like.'

In spite of his encouraging words June remained very uneasy. Being late was only one of her problems. What was

Harley going to say when he saw Emily? Had Agnes been fabricating the tale about Harley and Emily? It looked rather like it after that unfriendly farewell. The girl had been making a nuisance of herself and Agnes had welcomed the chance to get rid of her. That seemed the most probable explanation. June had the strong suspicion that she had been taken in by the cunning of Agnes Rowley. Some women do behave strangely when they are pregnant, she told herself reassuringly. Then with a qualm of doubt added, Will that be a good enough reason for Doctor Tretton?

It was nearly eleven o'clock when they drove into the camp. And by that time June was feeling so weary that she scarcely cared what Harley said. It had been a hard and uncomfortable journey for Bill had to drive much more slowly because of the darkness. Halfway back the truck had run off the track and smashed one of the front lamps and they had had to proceed with even more caution. Added to that Emily had wept copiously for most of the trip and June had exhausted herself with trying to comfort her. Even Bill had become morose and when he reached the camp was thankful that he could relinquish his mission of goodwill.

The canteen was in darkness but lamps glowed in some of the cabins as they drove towards the Mission House. Evidently they had been heard for Harley came out of the Mission as they were climbing down stiffly from the truck.

'Where the heck have you been?' he shouted angrily at Bill. 'I was about to send out a search party.'

'I'm sorry, Doc,' Bill said placatingly. 'One of the front lamps got smashed. It slowed us up.'

'Not all that much, surely! Why didn't you leave earlier?' He turned on June who was sagging against the truck waiting for his anger to abate. 'Nurse Bentley! You were in charge. Why ...?' He broke off as he caught sight of Emily's slim figure. 'Is something wrong? What brings you here, Emily?'

Because Emily seemed too stricken to answer June stepped forward and remarked quietly, 'Could we discuss this inside, Doctor? We are all very tired.'

'Okay. I guess there's no point in arousing the rest of the camp.'

June looked at Bill who had been awkwardly waiting for the chance to leave. 'Thanks for taking me, Bill,' she said. 'I'm sorry it was a rough trip.'

'My pleasure, Nurse. I have to be up early so I will be off now.' He disappeared into the darkness leaving the truck where he had parked it.

'Come along Emily!' June took the girl's arm. 'You will feel better when you've had some coffee. Doctor Tretton will carry your case.'

June sensed that it was the final straw as far as Harley was concerned but she was too weary to bother about being tactful. With ill-concealed bad humour Harley picked up the case and stalked into the Mission House behind the two girls.

'Emily, you come with me,' June said as she walked across to the clinic and through to her own room. 'There you are! You can use this room. Make yourself comfortable. I will bring the coffee in to you after I've explained to the doctor.'

The moment she had been dreading had arrived. After closing the bedroom door June went back to Harley who was staring into space with a black scowl on his face.

She hesitated then seeing no point in prolonging the agony said firmly, 'I'm sorry we kept you up, Doctor. I didn't intend to be so late. I hope there weren't any emergencies.'

'Lucky for you there weren't,' he said irritably. 'I reckon you didn't spare a thought for my state of mind. Anything could have happened.'

'Well nothing did. I can't see why you should be so put out.'

'I can see that! Your unconcern is darn aggravating.'

'I'm sorry,' she said uneasily.

'Quit apologizing! It's not helping. I'm waiting to hear how you got on.'

'Oh, we had an enjoyable day. We arrived about eleven o'clock. After that the time flew by.' She flicked a curious glance at him. 'What made you send Chris there?'

He shrugged his broad shoulders indifferently. 'It seemed logical to get you two together. He turned up then? Is that what kept you?'

'No. Chris didn't stay long. I would like to thank you doctor. It was a nice thought.'

'No thanks necessary,' he said gruffly. 'It was a purely selfish move. You know as well as I do, Nurse that in our profession personal problems can play havoc with our work. The way you have been looking lately I knew I had to do something.'

She smiled wryly. 'I see. I had no idea it was affecting my duties.'

'I didn't say it was but it might have eventually. Perhaps now we can settle down without any emotional upsets.'

The silence which followed seemed interminable until June remarked quietly, 'I've settled your problem about Mrs Rowley. She's agreed to go to hospital. I said you would make all the arrangements.'

His face looked less severe. 'She's going to be sensible? Then some good did come of your trip.' He paused then added gruffly. 'My thanks, Nurse. I'm grateful.'

'I was only too pleased to be able to help.'

He asked abruptly, 'Why has Emily come here?'

June moistened her lips, took a few seconds to consider how she could explain it, then said carefully, 'Mrs Rowley said the girl needed a change of scene. She hasn't been too well and has become bored with the homestead. Agnes asked me if Emily could stay with me for awhile. I didn't like to refuse.'

'Why not?'

'Mrs Rowley had given in about going to hospital. I thought I owed her something. I don't mind having Emily with me. She can have my room.'

'Where are you going to sleep? I can't allow you to use a cabin.'

'I don't intend to. I can sleep in the clinic.'

Expecting further protest she was very surprised when he said equably, 'Good idea. I guess there's no reason why Emily can't stay. She will be company for you. She's a real nice girl. I'm surprised that Agnes allowed her to leave. I thought the reason she came up north was to keep her aunt from working too hard.'

'I gathered that Mrs Rowley prefers to be on her own.' June spoke awkwardly.

Harley looked at her intently. 'You think Agnes was making excuses to get rid of her?'

'I couldn't be certain. It was just a feeling I had. I noticed Emily looked unhappy but she was very upset when she left. That didn't seem to tie in with what her aunt said.'

'I've had my suspicions myself. It's a real shame. Emily's mother sent her away because she had got herself into some scrape or other. At least that's what Agnes told me. How could a girl like that be a nuisance?' Harley smiled for the first time that evening. 'You were right to bring her back with you. You may find her useful. Let her stay until she suggests she go. I would like to do something for the girl.'

June nodded. 'Will you have a cup of coffee with us, Doctor?' she asked politely thinking that Agnes had been right about Harley being attracted to Emily.

'No, it's too late.' He paused to give her a severe glance. 'You look exhausted! It's time you hit the hay.'

June was not sorry to see him go. She had the sheets to change and another bed to make up. Emily was curled up on top of the bed when June went into her room and it took a certain amount of vigorous shaking to wake her. But after drinking the coffee she revived enough to help June with the beds.

It was nearly midnight when they turned out the lamps. June fell asleep as soon as her head touched the pillow and she did not open her eyes until the first gong sounded for breakfast.

CHAPTER FIVE

Three days passed quickly. Emily seemed much happier, evidently enjoying the fuss that was made of her. She soon became friendly with the men and spent most of the day chatting to them either in the canteen or outside their cabins. June felt a little nervous at first because the girl was apparently fearless but gradually she accustomed herself to seeing Emily in the company of different men and realized that she was well able to look after herself. One thing was certain she was becoming very popular and life in the camp seemed brighter.

It did not take June long to discover why Agnes had been so eager to get rid of her niece. The girl was good-tempered and willing but not blessed with much intelligence. This made her clumsy and awkward and June found it was quicker and easier to do things herself. A certain amount of tact had to be constantly used and after a time June began to tire and it took all her patience to endure Emily's obtuseness. Luckily Harley did not appear to notice and obviously enjoyed having Emily tag after him when he went to visit the men in camp and told June that he was delighted that the girl took such pleasure in trivial things.

My first impression was right, June thought, feeling for some unknown reason rather dismayed. He does like her a lot. Emily's very pretty. Perhaps she doesn't appear dull to men. Well he's perfectly free to choose her if he wants to, she reminded herself sternly. But it is astonishing! I thought he disliked women. Guy hinted that he had been disappointed in love. If that was so, it looks very much as if he's got over it.

Emily called him Harley and childishly

raised her rounded cheek to receive a light kiss first thing in the morning. June pretended not to notice and hid her embarrassment. Harley took it in his stride evidently not noticing June's reaction to the oddity of the situation.

But try as she might June found it difficult to remain on a friendly level with Harley and consequently her coolness soon became apparent. What have I done now? Harley asked himself irritably. I can't venture two words to June without her shutting up like a clam. And the way she looks at me sometimes! It's not my fault that her fiancé is unable to see her more often. I thought that arranged meeting would have cleared things up between them.

If June had but known it her cold manner only made Harley turn more frequently to Emily for companionship. With her he did not have to pretend. And it was good to feel she liked being with him. That she had nothing to do all day did not worry him. June could have told him that Emily spent hours dressing, combing her hair and manicuring her nails. He only saw the result and found it very satisfying to have such a pretty young thing at his elbow and enjoyed the envious glances he got from the men when he strolled about with her.

Annoyed with herself for allowing Emily and Harley to upset her June worked industriously. Taking one section at a time she cleared the waiting-room, clinic and surgery and gave them a good clean. Harley grumbled because his room had been disturbed but June ignored his protest saying crisply that it was high time something was moved. And the only satisfaction she gained from her activities was the praise of the men when they attended the clinic.

'Never seen it like this before,' one man said, his face reflecting his admiration. 'How did you get it all to shine like this, Nurse?'

June smiled and flicked a glance at

Harley who was standing at the door of his surgery. He shrugged his shoulders and disappeared inside so June missed the amused smile on his lips.

Emily wanted to help with the patients but June firmly resisted her offers. The clinic was her territory and Harley was the only one allowed to work in there. How could she dress men's wounds with Emily at her elbow knocking things over and distracting the patients?

Emily took it in good part after Harley had suggested that she leave June to cope by herself. She never argued with Harley and that perhaps was why he enjoyed having her around.

There was one great advantage of having Emily in the camp and June soon made use of it. There was no shower room in the Mission and before Emily arrived she had to lock herself in the clinic when she wanted to take a bath. The men were luckier for they bathed in the river which supplied the camp with water. June had often visited the fast flowing, clear waters which tumbled down from the rocks to a stony bed before disappearing into the dark forest. The stream had looked so inviting but because there had always seemed to be someone there when she went she reluctantly decided to keep away.

Now with Emily for support she went there regularly to bathe. The days had become much warmer since she had arrived for May had given them a spell of bright sunny weather. The water was icy and too shallow to swim in but it was invigorating and with one girl to keep watch whilst the other bathed it became fairly safe to use the place.

Coming back from their bathe one morning they were startled to see Harley running down the steps of the Mission House. He was wearing oil-rig clothes and carried his doctor's case.

'What's happened?' June exclaimed. 'Why are you dressed like that?'

'Joe sent for me. There's been a riot in

the new camp. This gear will protect my clothes. Oil isn't easy to remove.'

'A riot! Does that mean the men have been fighting?' she asked in astonishment.

'That's right.' He looked impatient. 'Don't delay me! I have to get over there.'

'Can I come with you?'

He frowned. 'It's no place for you. Joe says it's like a battlefield out there. Scarcely any of the men are uninjured. One of them is seriously hurt.'

Emily gasped, 'That's awful! Perhaps I could help?'

June interrupted quickly. 'If it's as bad as that you will need me. I can come as I am. It doesn't matter about my clothes.'

'If it means I'm going to get away quickly, okay,' Harley said. 'Come on, I haven't time to argue!' He turned his back on them and strode towards the jeep.

'If you want to help, Emily, prepare as many beds as you can,' June said before she ran after the doctor.

June waited until Harley had driven the jeep through the camp before she asked nervously, 'Did Joe say which man is seriously injured?'

'One of the crew bosses,' he replied without looking at her.

June's face whitened. 'There's only two. Is it Andy or Chris?'

He slowed down and gave her a swift glance. 'You okay? You sure look pale.'

'Yes. Don't stop. I will be all right.'

'Joe didn't say which one. He was in a hurry to get back. He brought three men in with him. I've seen to them. They only had minor injuries.'

'Where are they now?'

'They went back with Joe to help clear up the mess.'

'It does sound bad.'

Harley did not answer. He was concentrating on driving the jeep as fast as possible. They had a long way to go and every minute was precious. June closed her eyes grappling with the fear that

Andy might die. No not that, she prayed. Then guiltily she reminded herself that it might be Chris who had been badly hurt. I don't want it to be him either, she told herself unhappily. This is awful! How can I choose like this when one of them may be dying.

'Buck up, Nurse! It may not be as serious as you think,' Harley said when they reached a straight stretch of road. 'Joe has medical supplies out there and Reg, one of the men knows how to use them. If I hadn't known that I would have gone sooner and left you to cope with the injured men Joe brought in.'

'Do you often have fights in these camps?'

'Sure but not on such a big scale as this. Apparently the two crews went for each other.' He broke off then said carelessly. 'Andy and Chris don't hit it off too well, do they?'

'They were close friends before they came to Smoky River. The three of us emigrated together. Now they can't agree over anything.'

'Why is that?'

'I can't understand it at all. Andy is so good-tempered usually. Naturally he does flare up sometimes but it never lasts. And Chris ought to be used to him by now. Andy says Chris has changed. He takes his work very seriously especially since he's been made a crew boss.'

'The jealousy between the two bosses evidently influenced their crews. A few harsh words were said and the men flew at one another. It will finish Andy and Chris working together.'

They did not speak much after that. June felt too numbed with anxiety and Harley was intent on getting to the camp. Luckily the road was a faster one than the dirt lane to the Rowley's homestead for it had been used frequently by heavy trucks. They saw the tall oil derrick some time before they reached the drilling rig catching glimpses of it between breaks in the forest where the timber had been cleared.

Then they were out of the jeep and ankle deep in moist, red soil. Harley took no notice for he was used to such conditions and was wearing high heavy boots. And after a few minutes June disregarded the discomfort for there was too much to claim her attention. The gleaming silver derrick on a raised platform and the huge red machinery scattered below it drew her notice first. The wooden steps and supports to the derrick and a large area around it were covered with pipes and poles of great length. Some had obviously been disturbed for piles of debris cluttered the earth between the huts and the rest of the clearing.

A band of dark green forest encircled the field but the trees close to the derrick showed trunks bared and scarred by flame and fumes. A few men were operating the rig but many more were running to and from the huts looking very agitated. June kept close to Harley who was ploughing his way towards the largest hut. They had nearly reached it when Joe came out and walked over to them.

'The injured men are in the first hut,' he explained giving June a nod and a faint smile. 'Good of you to come, Nurse. We can sure do with any help we can get.'

'Is my brother hurt?' she asked nervously.

'No. Andy is okay except for a few bruises and cuts.'

June felt a little ashamed of the relief which swept over her. Aware that Harley was giving her a curious look she made a tremendous effort to speak calmly.

'What do you want me to do first, Doctor?'

'Come with me,' he said curtly and swinging his case marched on ahead.

Reg smiled at them as they entered the hut and drew Harley aside so that he could explain briefly how badly each man was hurt. 'I've patched them up as best I can but you ought to check. None of them are fatally injured. Ferris has some

156

nasty knife wounds. I think you ought to examine him first.'

'Okay, Reg. It looks as if you've coped real well. Nurse, you attend to the other men. Reg can help me with Ferris.'

Grateful for his consideration for it would have been painful and unnerving to have had to attend to Chris, June made a start on the men who were injured the most. Some, the ones in less pain gave her sheepish glances and she guessed that they were beginning to feel ashamed of the way they had behaved. She worked swiftly and finished applying dressings, slings and splints before Harley had finished with Chris.

A few of the men got up and went out staggering a little as they moved determinedly to the door. June smiled to herself as she watched them go. She had advised them to rest but they were a tough bunch and a few sprains, bruises and cuts would not keep them inside.

With anxiety she remembered Chris and

moved to the end of the hut where Harley and Reg were attending to him. She watched them silently, fear gripping her heart as she noted the greyness of Chris's face beneath the bulky head bandage.

Harley glanced up at her. His face tightened and his eyes became bleak as he noticed her pale strained face.

'Don't worry. He looks worse than he is,' he said quickly.

June moistened her dry lips. 'Has he spoken to you?'

'No. We didn't give him the chance. We had to give him an injection. He has five knife wounds and we had to dress them. The pain would have been too much for him.'

'Are any of them serious?' she asked nervously.

'They might have been without prompt attention. He was darn lucky. Someone cut his head open with some heavy object. We've stitched the wound. It ought to heal without too bad a scar.' He gazed at her steadily. 'Don't look so upset. He's going to be okay.'

The relief eased her guilt as well as her anxiety and she breathed more easily after that. Then seeing that they did not need her she left them to go and search for Andy. She found him clearing away the debris from the base of the derrick. His left arm was in a sling, his head was bandaged and he was limping.

'Joe said you weren't hurt!' she exclaimed unable to hide the smile of amusement at his bizarre appearance.

He grinned. 'Reg does rather overdo the treatment. A small dressing was all that was needed on my head. It's only a scratch.'

'I'm glad to hear it. What's wrong with your arm?'

He pulled it from the sling and showed her the swollen knuckles of his hand which was black with bruises. 'It's too stiff to use. It feels better tucked out of the way.'

'What about your limp?'

'Twisted ankle, that's all. Nothing to worry about.'

She chuckled. 'That's what they have all been saying. I'm beginning to suspect that they enjoyed the fight.'

He grinned. 'You could be right. Anyway it certainly cleared the air.'

'Chris might not agree with that. He's the one most seriously hurt.'

Andy became grave. 'Yes. I'm sorry about that. So many men went for him I didn't have the chance to help him.'

'So you didn't start it?'

'Good heavens, no! Surely you didn't think that! Chris often makes me see red but I wouldn't go so far as to attack him with a knife! No, he laid down the law a bit too drastically and one of his crew went for him. He picked up a short pole to defend himself and the others began to join in. It wasn't until I saw the knives flashing about that it dawned on me that it was serious. Two of my men and myself managed to drag Chris away. We had to fight our way across to the hut where we locked him inside. The others turned on us then but they had no reason to fight us so it gradually died down.'

'So Chris really brought it on himself.'

'I've been watching it coming for a long time. I told you he had changed. The responsibility turned his head. He really enjoyed ordering the men about. But having power over others ought not to mean dictatorship. The men resented his arrogance and the bossy way he talked to them. None of them liked him.'

'But to use knives!' June exclaimed. 'Surely that was unnecessary?'

'These men are different to any you have been used to, Sis. They come from different nationalities, are extremely strong and some have violent tempers. Self preservation is always uppermost in their minds.'

June smiled ruefully. 'I'm beginning to understand Doctor Tretton's preference for male assistance.'

Andy frowned. 'Has he been giving you a rough time?'

'Oh no,' she replied hastily. 'He's resigned himself to having to put up with me. It hasn't been too bad. I was only thinking of when he first saw me. He was furious with Guy and he made it quite clear that I wouldn't be of any use to him.'

'I bet he's changed his opinion now.' Andy smiled. 'You are very efficient and easy to get on with besides being easy on the eye. How's that recommendation coming from a brother?'

She laughed. 'Too good to be true. I doubt whether the doctor would agree.'

'He's not a bad sort. He's the only man apart from Joe whom the men respect.'

'I don't envy Joe. How is he going to explain about the fight to Guy Burleigh? Has the derrick been damaged?'

'No, but the company will lose money. Guy won't like that. As for myself I'm not sorry it has happened. Joe has looked worried for some days. He warned Chris to ease up and not push his men so hard. Chris never could take advice. He became angry and took it out on his men. Now Joe will have to find another crew boss. He won't take Chris back.'

'He's going to be awfully upset. What will he do?'

'I couldn't care less,' Andy retorted roughly. 'I'm sorry, June. I know you want to marry him but I've had enough of Chris to last me a lifetime. If you have any sense you will finish with him before it's too late. I regret that he's been badly hurt but we are all going to breathe more freely with him out of the way.'

June frowned. 'It's not that simple. But I can understand your sentiments. It can't have been easy for you. I won't hinder you any longer, Andy. I know you have plenty to do. Come into Smoky River camp and pay me a visit when you can spare the time.'

June left him intending to find Harley to see if he wanted her assistance. Most of the men working on the clearing had patches of dressings on their heads, arms in slings and some even had their legs bandaged up to the knee. A few gave her a friendly grin or spoke to her and none as far as she could see were angry or belligerent. Some of them were whistling as they marched by with huge poles resting on their shoulders and one huge, fair-haired giant was noisily singing an aria. They are behaving like naughty boys recovering from an attack of bad temper, June thought and laughed quietly to herself. I can see why Chris doesn't fit in. He's much too stiff and proper. It will take him years to get used to conditions here. I can see that the men really enjoy their work. Chris must have made them feel like a labour gang.

Two trucks were drawn up close to the hut June had left a short time before and the injured men were being helped into one of them. June quickly moved across to Harley who was assisting a man with an injured leg.

'How many are you taking back?' she asked.

'Seven, including Ferris. Have you seen your brother?'

'Yes. He's all right. And as far as I can see the rest of the men are eager to start work again.'

'It could have been worse. You can travel with me in the other truck, Nurse. We will put Ferris in there.'

'You are keeping him apart from the others?'

'It's safer. I don't want any trouble on the way back.'

June frowned. 'Surely they wouldn't attack him in that condition?'

'There's no telling what they might do. Some are badly injured and they blame Ferris. A couple of them have threatened to get even with him.'

'That sounds bad.' June looked worried.

'How are we going to cope with them in the Mission?'

'I've asked Joe if we can have Reg for a spell.' Harley grinned. 'No need to look so downcast. I would have done the same if I had had a male assistant. With three of us keeping an eye on them I doubt whether we shall have another fight. Some of them won't be in camp too long. With a little care they will be back at work in a few days.'

Chris had recovered consciousness but he was still drowsy from the drugs he had been given and held June's hand tightly throughout the journey back. If she had not known the injured man she would not have taken any notice, thinking it her duty to give him what comfort she could. But with Harley sitting there staring at them grimly, it seemed a very long and uncomfortable trip and she was infinitely relieved when they reached the Mission House.

He even looked annoyed with Emily

when he discovered that she had made no attempt to make up the beds.

'I didn't know how many you would want,' she said apologetically. 'I did get some sheets and blankets ready. I've put them on top of the bed over there.'

'Okay,' he said curtly. 'It was too much to expect, I guess.' He turned to June who was mentally calculating how many sheets they would need and brought her to attention by saying sharply, 'You take over, Nurse. Make a bed up for Ferris first and be as quick as you can.'

June worked swiftly ignoring Emily's offer to help. The girl was willing but she would only have hindered the bed-making. As it was June was hard put to keep up with the flow of injured men whom Reg was bringing in. And by the time all the men were tucked up comfortably June felt utterly exhausted. It's a pity Emily is so useless, she thought tiredly as she went into the clinic to scrub her hands. Many hands are supposed to make light work but not in this case. I wonder how she got by at home? I bet her mother never let her help. All the same she felt a little sorry for the girl who was sitting in her room to keep out of the way and went in to have a chat with her after she had finished in the clinic.

But June was very grateful for Emily's companionship during the next few days. Surprisingly enough the girl became very useful in keeping the men occupied whilst June attended to them. Expecting trouble June had wondered how they would cope if the men turned nasty and quarrelled with Chris. But with Emily sitting on their beds chatting away and keeping their minds on her they had little time to become belligerent. June was amazed at the girl's confidence as she listened to the men's problems, played cards with them and patiently picked up the items that continually fell off their beds.

'Emily, bless her heart, has saved the day,' Harley remarked one evening after he had finished examining the men. 'We've had no trouble so far and if Emily can keep them from nursing their resentment we ought to ride the storm. Ferris is improving daily and I can discharge three of the men in a couple of days.'

'Yes,' June said thoughtfully. 'It's never wise to judge anyone too soon. Emily has been wonderful. I really don't know what I would have done without her.'

'You thought she was useless?'

'Not entirely,' June smiled as she quoted, ' "If eyes were made for seeing, then Beauty is its own excuse for being." '

Harley stared at her raising his thick eyebrows in astonishment. 'How come you know Waldo Emerson?'

'I often read poetry. I bought a small volume of American poems in Vancouver. I found Emerson stimulating and those particular lines stuck in my mind.'

'I never cease to be surprised at you. Yes, the quotation fits Emily well. She's mighty different to you,' he said eyeing her

169

thoughtfully. 'We couldn't do without the Emily's of this world. They help us over the rough spots.'

June turned away quickly, afraid that he would notice the hurt in her eyes. Not that she did not agree with his remark. It was just that she would have welcomed a word of appreciation. The last few days had been a tremendous strain for she had had the brunt of the work, tending the men, washing them, dressing their wounds and supervising their meals. Reg had been unable to help her for Chris had been his chief concern. Doctors never do notice how much a nurse does in the course of a day, she reminded herself. It's nothing unusual. At the General I would have other nurses to listen to my grumbles and be able to let off steam. Here I have to bottle it all up. Emily has been a disappointment. It's no use talking to her. She doesn't understand and no wonder when she never does anything to exert herself.

June had not thought it possible that she

could ever welcome Guy warmly but when he did breeze in oozing self importance she sensed a breath of normality returning to the camp. With him came a reminder of the outside world and the tension and petty misunderstandings of the few days since the fight took on their true prospective. She might have thought that she alone was irritable and touchy had it not been for the fact that Harley was continually snapping at herself and Reg.

Reg mentioned Harley's surly manner one day to June. 'What's eating him?' he grumbled. 'There's nothing wrong with the set-up. The patients are behaving themselves and Chris is doing fine. What's Harley got to be grumpy about?'

June frowned. 'I was beginning to think I was the only one to notice it but if he is upsetting you then it can't be because I'm feeling touchy.'

'If you are you never show it,' Reg said with a smile. 'I've seen guys like that before and there was always a woman who was responsible. I reckon it might be different with Harley. Emily dotes on him. She wouldn't lead him a dance. I can't figure him out at all. Perhaps he's scared to take the plunge. It gets guys like that sometimes.'

'You could be right,' June said slowly suddenly aware of a blanket of gloom enveloping her. 'He does think highly of Emily but he was disappointed in love a few years back.'

'That's it then! Why the heck doesn't he get a grip on himself and settle things with her?' Reg said irately. 'The atmosphere in the Mission could be cut with a knife.'

'I'm going to change out of this dress,' June said quickly, unable to continue talking about Harley without revealing how miserable she was feeling. 'Can you carry on here for a few minutes?'

'Sure, take your time. You look real tired, June. Harley expects you to do too much.'

June put on jeans and a white sweater

for it was late afternoon and the evenings had a habit of becoming chilly. Then she went for a breath of air making the most of the break to get away from the Mission for a few minutes. And it was as she was walking across the clearing that she ran into Guy Burleigh.

If he was surprised by the warmth of her greeting he did not show it. 'What have you been up to, Nurse?' he asked jovially. 'I've had reports of riots, sabotage and skirmishes.'

She smiled. 'If you did it's an exaggeration. There was a fight but it was soon over.'

'Harley and Joe have told me their side. I would be interested to hear yours, Nurse.'

'I don't think I ought to discuss it. I know very little.'

'Ferris is your fiancé isn't he? Aren't you interested in his future?'

She nodded her head. 'What's going to happen to him?'

'I ought to fire him. That's what I usually do with trouble-makers. Joe says he didn't set out to cause trouble but I can't excuse him on that score. He's cost the company money and we can't have that, can we? I could send him to another camp but it wouldn't be as a crew boss. I couldn't trust him again. How would he take being demoted?'

'You will have to ask him that. I imagine he won't like it.'

'Didn't think he would. No the simplest thing is to ask him to seek employment elsewhere. I will give him a good reference. There's nothing wrong with his work. Your brother now, is of different mettle. I wouldn't want to lose him. Is there a chance he would decide to keep Ferris company?'

'No. Andy wouldn't leave because of Chris.'

'That's okay then. Now I know what to do.'

June said nervously. 'Couldn't you

possibly send Chris to another camp? I'm sure he wouldn't make the same mistake.'

'As crew boss? No. I couldn't risk it, Nurse. I'm real sorry for you. It's real hard after you coming here especially to be with him. If you want to go with Ferris I shall understand but I would like you to stay. You seem to have done a good job here judging by the reports I've had.'

Becoming aware that Harley was striding towards them June began to move on but Guy called her back.

'Don't go, Nurse. What Harley and I have to say is not private.'

June reluctantly turned back and stood there uncertainly. Harley gave her a stony glance as he passed her.

'It's all over now, Guy,' he said curtly. 'I thought you might have come before this.'

'No doubt you did. I do have other camps to visit. Joe informed me that all was under control. I reckon it pays to let things simmer down. If the men see me snooping around they tend to imagine it's more serious than it is. I really came up to discuss Ferris' future. Why didn't you send him back to Grande Prairie? With his injuries he ought to have been in hospital.'

'I decide whom to send back. We settled that long ago, Guy. Ferris was badly hurt but he's mending fast. He ought to be on his feet in another week.' He gave June a cursory glance. 'I was thinking of Nurse Bentley's feelings. She came here to be with her fiancé and brother. It seemed unkind to inflict a parting so soon.'

Guy smiled sneeringly. 'Becoming sentimental, Harley?'

Harley's eyes narrowed. 'No. I prefer my assistant to keep her mind on her work. How could she do that with an injured fiancé miles away from her?'

'So your motive was selfish! I might have guessed.' Guy chuckled. 'When I first received the news that there had been a disturbance I reckoned that Nurse Bentley had something to do with it.'

'You were mighty disappointed, weren't you Guy?' Harley gave him a sour glance. 'The only tangles Nurse has had have been with me. We've kept her away from the other camps.'

'Is that a fact!' Guy smiled. 'Neither of you look as if you are enjoying the experience.' He turned to June and drawled. 'Does that mean you want to leave with Ferris?'

She hesitated her eyes troubled. 'If Doctor Tretton is dissatisfied then perhaps it would be the only thing to do.'

Guy said mockingly, 'There's your chance, Harley. Aren't you going to grab it?'

'No,' he said curtly. 'Stop badgering Nurse Bentley. There's no reason why either of them should go yet. I have four injured men to look after. Reg will have to return to his camp soon. He might be needed for minor accidents. Is there any reason why you want Ferris back in Grande Prairie? Do you intend to make an example of him?'

'No!' Guy sounded hurt. 'I won't even sack him if he agrees to be down-graded.'

'I can't see him doing that.'

'We shall see.' Guy smiled at June, 'Nurse may be able to influence him.'

June said nervously, 'I would rather not. Chris has to make up his own mind. If you will excuse me I ought to get back. I only came out for a few minutes.'

'If you change your mind about coming back, let me know,' Guy called after her. 'Real nice girl that,' he commented, his blue eyes glinting. 'I hope she decides to return.'

'You seem mighty keen to get her back to Grande Prairie,' Harley said roughly.

'Why not? An engagement is not as binding as a marriage. Any girl can change her mind. Why she might even make me decide to forsake my bachelor existence.'

Harley looked at him grimly. 'What

makes you so darn sure you have a chance?'

'She's too good for Ferris. Given the opportunity I would soon make her change her mind.'

'So that's the reason you want her back in Grande Prairie! Just the kind of behaviour I'd expect from you. Fool about with her whilst Ferris is in hospital and safely out of the way!'

'Real clever of you, Harley! I hadn't got that far but it's a good idea. For Pete's sake don't glower at me like that! I shall begin to think you have an interest in Nurse Bentley.'

'I have. I want to see her secure and happy. What are you going to do with Ferris?'

'Get rid of him eventually. He's no use to us. But keep your mouth shut. I don't want either Nurse Bentley or her fiancé to know.'

'You're a nasty piece of work, Guy. I can't think why I stay with you.'

179

'That's better. Now we're back to normal.' Guy smiled. 'From the look of you it might improve your temper if you took a leaf from my book. You might lose some of your frustration. By the way, who is the pretty creature ogling you from the Mission steps?'

Emily waved as Harley turned his head to glance back. He frowned darkly. 'Let her alone, Guy. She hasn't the stamina of Nurse Bentley. She's Mrs Rowley's niece. She's staying with us until Agnes comes in. If you remember I told you I'm sending her to Grande Prairie to have her child.'

Guy stared at the girl curiously. 'Why isn't she with her aunt?'

'She came to keep June company. It's lonely for her here.'

'Safety in numbers, eh?' Guy grinned. 'You're a cunning devil, Tretton. Sometimes I think I've met my match in you.'

'Think what you like,' Harley said carelessly. 'I'm well used to your devious mind but don't interfere.' And with that he turned away and walked swiftly back to the Mission.

Guy scowled. Insolent devil, he thought. Why don't I fire him and be done with it? Of course I would be cutting off my nose to spite my face. He's a first class doctor and it's difficult to get medical men. I don't have to see him that often. If I had to like all our employees I wouldn't have many left. I never did care for the men who work in the camps. They are too darned independent. Still frowning he made his way to the truck which was waiting to take him to the landing field.

'Who was that?' Emily asked when Harley reached her.

'One of the Partners. He's going back to Grande Prairie now.' He gave her an enquiring glance. 'You could have gone with him, you know. You don't have to stay here.'

Emily shook her head. 'No. I can't go back yet. I like it here. Gosh that

181

man was smart! I wouldn't have minded meeting him.'

'He'd be no good for you.' Harley smiled and put his arm across her shoulders as they went into the Mission. June saw them come in and was astonished at the sharp thrust of pain in the region of her heart as she saw them so close. Harley was smiling indulgently at Emily but when he glanced at June his expression changed. I'd give anything for him to look at me like that, she reflected wistfully. Before Emily came we were good friends. What's happened? Why is he so hostile towards me now?

She was supervising the evening meal and had left Chris until last because he needed assistance with his feeding. Harley left Emily and went across to watch June spooning the food into Chris' mouth. June felt herself becoming nervous with Harley standing there watching them silently. Chris was hating being the object of their pity and tried to take the spoon in his bandaged hands.

'Here, let me take over,' Harley said. 'Neither of you are doing much good. There's no point in messing up your bandages, Chris. June will only have to do them again.'

'I don't want any more to eat,' Chris said irritably. 'How much longer have I got to stay in bed?'

'Until next week. You have recovered quickly. I know it's tedious lying here with nothing to do, but it's necessary, believe me. Guy wants you to go to hospital if you don't improve.'

'I don't care. I want to get out of this place,' Chris muttered.

June put her hand on his shoulder. 'Why Chris? Is something bothering you?' she asked gently. 'Is there anything I can do?'

'Yes!' he said sharply. 'Go away and leave me alone. I can't stand your pity.'

She blinked then with a downcast face picked up the dish and left him making her way swiftly to the clinic. She was washing the spoon and dish when Harley strode in.

'Sympathy won't help him,' he said. 'He's got to snap out of it. It's getting so he's afraid to open his eyes in the morning.'

'I know.' She wiped her hands on a towel and turned to face him. 'You don't understand. I feel responsible. If it hadn't been for me none of it would have happened.'

He stared, his lips curving into a smile. 'That's ridiculous. He has only himself to blame.'

'I knew you wouldn't understand. I can't explain. I'm worried about him. He's so despondent and unsure of himself. It's so unlike him.'

'He's had a traumatic experience. It's given him a shock. Eventually it might improve his outlook. He can't walk over people all his life.'

'You make him sound so ...'

'Selfish? Well he is, isn't he? Come on

now, admit it! Look how he treated you.'

'He's different now. He doesn't mind about being fired. I've discussed it with him. He's decided to return to England.'

'What about you?' Harley's grey eyes were concerned.

She was silent for a few moments then said expressionlessly, 'He wants me to go with him.'

Harley drew in his breath and his face paled. He took a step forward, grasped her wrists and tightened his fingers as she tried to evade him. 'You can't do that!' he exclaimed roughly. 'Why should you agree to everything he wants?' Then controlling his voice with an effort, he went on, 'Do think carefully before you decide. Smoky River won't seem the same without you and Emily and I will miss you.'

June remained silent, too distressed to pretend. Then as the pressure on her wrists increased she gazed straight into his grey eyes and asked quietly, 'If you were Chris what would you expect me to do?'

He jerked as if from shock, dropped his hands and stepped away from her. 'That's not a fair question,' he said gruffly. 'I guess I would hope that you would stick by me.'

'Thank you, Doctor Tretton.'

'Why?' He turned on her fiercely. 'Is it because I've helped you to make up your mind?'

'No.' Her blue eyes clouded with unhappy thoughts. 'I've already done that. You merely confirmed my decision.'

Taut and with a baffled expression on his face he stood watching her at a loss as to what to do or say.

June said awkwardly, 'You have been very good to Chris. I do appreciate what you have done for him.'

He shrugged his broad shoulders. 'He was a patient. I would have done the same for anyone.' Reaching the door, he turned before he opened it and glanced back at her. 'Whatever you do you can count on me to help in any way I can.'

The room seemed strangely quiet and empty after he had gone. In danger of collapsing June sat down in a chair and clasped her hands together, willing herself to cease trembling. 'Emily and I' ... the words burned into her mind. He is serious about the girl ... she thought. He wouldn't have mentioned her if he hadn't been thinking of her. He believes Emily needs me. He's sorry for her. No wonder I don't care for Chris any more, she told herself with ruthless honesty. How can I when it's Harley I love. I've never ceased thinking about him since that time he was so kind to me after Andy told me Chris was finished with me. And I never really understood until now. I was so mixed up about Chris and what I ought to do. How strange! It just crept up on me. No wonder I was jealous of Emily!

She sighed and got to her feet thankful that she had not revealed how she felt about Harley. That would have been embarrassing, she thought with a wry smile. At least I've spared him that!

But there were too many tasks to be finished before she could allow herself the luxury of self reflection. One thing was very clear. She could not remain at Smoky River camp feeling the way she did. She would go with Chris when he left but not back to England. That she could not bring herself to do. Chris did not love her. He had made that very plain. But he did need her support whilst he was ill. That in all loyalty she could and would give. She owed him that much. Afterwards she would go her own way; make a new life for herself. There were plenty of opportunities for nursing.

She finished cleaning up in the clinic, asked Emily to keep an eye on the patients and walked across to the canteen for her evening meal. Emily usually went with Harley so she had no qualms about leaving the girl alone. For a few days she was determined not to dwell on the unhappy state of her heart. Outwardly nothing had changed. She was Doctor Tretton's assistant and she had gained the respect of the men. That fact was comforting and did much to restore her self confidence.

CHAPTER SIX

It was sunny and warm the next day. June, feeling depressed, would have preferred it to rain. It would have been more in keeping with her mood. She went about her duties looking very subdued. Chris being too wrapped up in his own misery did not notice but Harley did and wished he could do something to cheer her up.

'Have you had breakfast, Nurse?' he asked intercepting her as she was walking across to Chris.

'Not yet. I was giving the men their meal first.' She glanced up at him and smiled. 'They have enormous appetites.'

'Yes. There's not much wrong with them now. How about Ferris? Is he eating well?'

'No.' She hesitated then went on, 'I

suppose Reg couldn't stay a little longer? Chris doesn't like me feeding him.'

'Sorry that's not possible. Reg has to leave today.' Harley took the tray from her. 'Leave him to me in future.' He stared at her thoughtfully for a few moments then said carelessly. 'I'm not doing much this morning. You take the morning off. It's a beautiful day. Where's Emily?'

'Still in bed I think.'

Harley smiled. 'You can do something about that. Take her to the river after you have had breakfast. Then report back here at one o'clock.'

He did not wait for her to thank him but moved quickly across to Chris who was sitting up in bed with a morose expression on his face. June watched Harley put down the tray and saw that Chris had brightened up a little and sighed to herself. Chris really is a puzzle she thought as she walked into the clinic and through to Emily's room. He's asked me to go back with him yet he can't bear me near him. If only he

191

wasn't so proud! Other men have to put up with the humiliation of being tended to by a nurse. I knew he hated hospitals but I never realized how deep his aversion was. Yet Reg and Harley seem to deal with him without any fuss. Perhaps it's just me he's against. I know I annoyed him by coming to Smoky River but he ought to have got over that by now.

Emily was dressing when June knocked on the door and opened it. She smiled sheepishly and began to hurry, pulling a red sweater over her golden head with a jerk.

'I overslept. Why didn't you bang on my door?' she asked. 'I sure hope Harley isn't here yet.'

'He is but don't let that bother you. He says I can have the morning off. How about coming with me for a bathe after breakfast?'

'Sure, I would like that. I never seem to get much of your company. You are always so busy.'

'I do have to work. That's what I get paid for.'

'Sure, I know. I wasn't blaming you. I guess it's not so lonely for me here as it was at the homestead. There's always someone I can talk to.'

June smiled. 'We shall have heaps of time for that today. You can tell me all about yourself, Emily. I would be very interested to hear about your life at home.'

'You would? Gee, that's real nice of you. It might help me to sort myself out.'

'I wouldn't have thought you needed to do that! You seem such an uncomplicated person.'

'Is that a fact? Yet if there's any bother around it always drifts across to me.'

Harley nodded to them as they walked through the waiting-room and the men whistled shrilly. Emily stopped to speak to them but June urged her away.

'We shall be too late for breakfast if

we don't hurry,' she explained good-humouredly.

'Gee whiz, I'm sorry. It's my tongue. It will run away with me.'

The canteen was about to close as they reached the door but the cook stretched a point and served them with cereal, toast and coffee. The girls ate and drank quickly then returned to the Mission House to collect towels and swimming suits. Emily went in for them on her own suggestion because she feared that Harley might decide he needed June for some task or other.

'No point in reminding him of your existence,' she drawled before she left.

'No point at all.' June smiled to herself. The remark was so very apt.

'Gosh, I thought I would never get away,' Emily exclaimed as she joined June.

'I thought you were a long time. What were you doing?'

'I couldn't find my towel and Harley insisted on finding another one for me. Gee, he's nice. He never minds what he does for me. Then we got talking. If Mr Ferris hadn't called out for him, I would be there still.'

'Shall we go farther down the river where it's deeper?' June asked. 'It's warm today. It would be good to be able to swim.'

'Sure I don't mind. I know where you mean. One of the men showed me where the river comes out of the forest. It's about half a mile the other side of camp.'

The girls were hot and tired by the time they reached the river and took a long time over their swim. And as no one was around to bother them they sat in the sun to dry their hair.

'Why did you really come up here, Emily?' June asked as she rubbed her hair gently.

The girl smiled. 'I reckon I knew you would ask me that. It wasn't to help my aunt. I guess you noticed she didn't want me.'

'I gathered you weren't very happy together.'

'No, we weren't.' Emily combed her golden hair and pushed it back from her smooth forehead. Her big brown eyes were wistful and she seemed young and very unsure of herself. 'Mom wanted me to get out of town for a while. She didn't approve of the company I was keeping.'

'You mean she didn't like your friends?' June asked curiously.

'One in particular; the boy who was dating me. She didn't dislike him, but it was awkward. You see he happened to be the son of my Pa's boss.'

'There was nothing wrong in that, surely? Didn't your parents approve of him?'

'They didn't mind. It was because his folk objected. They didn't think I was good enough for Herbie. He's their only child.'

'How unpleasant for you!'

'It sure was. Mrs Aberhart called on my Mom and made it real plain that they would never accept me at their house. I was to be told how foolish I was behaving in even thinking that I would ever be able to mix socially with their friends.'

June frowned. 'I don't like the sound of Mrs Aberhart. How did you react?'

Emily chuckled. 'I was mad. Oh boy, I was mad! And when I told Herbie, he was mad too.'

'What happened then? Did Herbie decide to stick by you?'

'I didn't give him the chance.' Emily had become very serious. 'At first I didn't understand how difficult it was for my Pa. You see we live in a small town a little way outside Grande Prairie. And it was only after Mrs Aberhart's visit that I noticed that people were talking about Herbie and me. Then when Mom said that we might have to move away because Pa would lose his job I knew I had to do something. Mom suggested that I come here and stay with Aunt Agnes. I guess I had acted pretty dumb until then but when I realized how rough on my folks it was going to be if I persisted in seeing

Herbie, I made up my mind to agree to come here.'

'Didn't you tell Herbie?'

'No. By that time I had stopped kidding myself that I was all that important to him. I left without seeing him.'

'That was a brave thing to do. Have you regretted it?'

Emily smiled. 'I was miserable at first. It might have been easier if Aunt Agnes had been more friendly. But I guess I sure got on her nerves. Then I met Harley and everything seemed all right again. Now I'm real glad I came.'

'He's made you forget Herbie?'

'I wouldn't say that. I shall never forget him. But what's the point of dwelling on what might have been. I like Harley a lot. He's different I guess. He makes me feel real nice. No one except Herbie ever made me feel I was a real person. My brother and sister knew I was pretty slow and shut me out. I guess a girl has to be smart to get anywhere. That's why meeting Herbie was really something. He didn't notice how dumb I was. How about that! That's really something, don't you think?'

June nodded and said softly, 'Brains aren't everything. And do you know something, Emily? I think you are a real nice girl.'

Emily laughed. 'Our slang sounds funny in your English accent.'

'Funny or not I meant it,' June said seriously.

Emily's face lit up. 'That's mighty nice of you. I wouldn't want to let Harley down. He's real clever.'

'I'm sure you won't. Shall we go back now? The sun is a little too hot for me. I'm not used to it.'

This enlightening conversation drew Emily and June closer together for June felt sorry for the girl and did not blame her for putting Harley in Herbie's place. Emily she decided was a brave little thing and it was about time she began to have a worthwhile life of her own. She had sacrificed her love to help her parents and had been rewarded by being treated as an outcast. Providence had sent Harley to that homestead, June thought and who am I to begrudge them their happiness. It's unfortunate that I also am in love with Harley but I have so much more than Emily. Perhaps happiness is too much to expect.

Without saying anything to Harley she sent a letter to Guy asking to be relieved of her duties at Smoky River camp and if it was convenient she would like to return with Chris Ferris the following week providing Doctor Tretton discharged him. She said nothing at first to Chris either, fearing that he might mention it to someone. It would be soon enough to tell Harley a few days before the plane left. She felt rather guilty about sending the letter because she knew that Guy would not have time to reply. He could radio a message through if he disagreed but she did not think he would do that. He can't refuse my request, June told herself confidently. I've been given no contract and he said I could go back if I wanted to. But she did send a note to Andy for she could not leave without seeing him.

Andy came into the camp a few days later. Chris had been up and about for the last two days and Harley had given him permission to fly back to Grande Prairie on the next plane which was expected in a couple of days time. June had told Chris that she was going with him but had not plucked up enough courage to inform Harley. It will be easier if I leave it until the last moment, she thought. He's sure to ask questions, some which I might find difficult to answer truthfully. Chris hasn't been exactly friendly towards me since he's been here and Harley will have noticed. Nothing slips by him and he will think it strange that I persist in hanging on to a man who doesn't want me. But Chris is the best excuse I have for leaving so suddenly. And it will simplify the situation. It would be very painful for me to stay on here having to watch Harley and Emily together.

Thinking that Andy would want a meal, the truck driver dropped him off outside the canteen. But Andy was too eager to see his sister and walked quickly across to the Mission House. Neither June nor Emily were there for they had gone to the river to bathe. Hearing this from an oil-man he knew who came out as Andy reached the steps, he hesitated then looking rather disappointed continued on into the waiting-room.

Harley had just finished examining his last patient, one of the men from Andy's camp.

'You are fit enough now, Fred,' he said with a smile. 'You can report back to Joe.' He glanced across at Andy. 'It looks as if a truck has come in so you're in luck. See that you have a meal before you go.'

'Thanks Doc. It's been a real nice change. I guess I'm going to miss the young ladies' company.'

Harley nodded and turned to Andy. 'What brings you here? I was congratulating myself that I had finished with the men from your outfit. Fred was our last one. All our beds are empty except for the one Chris has. There's nothing wrong with you I hope.'

Andy grinned. 'Not a thing. I came in to see my sister. She says she's leaving Smoky River.'

Harley had gone to the desk to place Fred's record card on it so Andy did not see his face or guess that he had given him a shock. And when Harley turned back his face was inscrutable.

'That's the first I've heard of it,' he said smoothly. 'Are you certain? It could be a rumour.'

Andy shook his head. 'I've got the note she sent me here.' He felt in his hip pocket and withdrew a soiled piece of paper. 'Yes, here we are. She says, "I've decided to go with Chris to Grande Prairie and as I'm not intending to return I would like to see you before I leave. Can you come soon? The plane will arrive next week". '

'That sounds conclusive.' Harley frowned. 'Why the heck didn't she tell me?' Thrusting his hands savagely into the pockets of his white jacket he began to pace the floor.

Andy glanced at him in a startled fashion. 'I'm sorry. I had no idea she hadn't discussed it with you. It looks as if I've thrown a spanner into the works. June will be furious with me.'

Harley smiled unpleasantly. 'She's left it as late as she could. The plane will come in any day now.'

'Do you know where she is?'

'She's gone off with Emily to bathe. They won't be long.'

'I will go and meet her,' Andy said quickly. 'I can't stay too long. The truck is going back in an hour.'

'You can tell your sister she has some explaining to do. I shall be waiting for her,' Harley said grimly.

Andy glanced at him uncertainly. 'Yes. I will do that.' He hesitated then said awkwardly, 'I can't understand why June hasn't told you. Doesn't she have to have your permission to leave?'

'I would have thought so.' Harley smiled twistedly. 'Your sister is relying on Mr Burleigh's co-operation. I was foolish enough to give her some good advice. Evidently she took it the wrong way. She didn't tell me of her decision because she anticipated some opposition.'

Andy smiled. 'She's very obstinate. If she makes up her mind that's that. Don't be too hard on her. Be seeing you, Harley; next time I'm in camp I expect. By the way where's Chris?'

'He's about somewhere,' the doctor said curtly. 'He pleases himself where he goes. He's another one who can't take advice.'

'Yes.' Andy looked at him doubtfully. 'He's not an easy guy to get on with. He's been a real disappointment to me.'

'Your sister evidently doesn't share your views,' Harley replied coldly.

'I can never tell with June. She's too darn loyal. Chris is lucky. I hope he appreciates what she is doing for him.'

Harley spoke jerkily, 'If you want to see her, get a move on! I would rather you didn't meet here.'

Andy nodded. 'Sure. I will make myself scarce. I haven't much time now.'

After Andy had gone banging the door behind him, Harley stood by the desk clenching and unclenching his hands abstractedly, his face creased with lines of anger and surprise. His grey eyes, cold as steel, hid the frustration but revealed the fury which consumed him. He remained there only a few minutes then tore off his white jacket and strode out of the Mission House, quickly gaining the cabin where the radio was installed. If Guy knows about this I want to know why he hasn't contacted me, he thought angrily. What am I here? Everyone's dupe!

June was delighted to see her brother. She had been feeling miserable and a little frightened since she had sent in her resignation and needed someone she knew well to talk to. Emily tactfully left them together and returned to the Mission House alone.

Harley came in soon after her. He looked angry and for the first time Emily felt afraid of him.

'Did you know that June was leaving?' he asked abruptly. He had been unable to contact Guy and had to lash out at someone.

'No,' she replied nervously, 'but I thought she might go soon.'

'Why?' he asked bluntly.

She moved uneasily. Harley seemed so unlike the man she was used to being with. 'I guess Chris is the reason. June told me he wasn't coming back. It figures that June would want to go also.'

'Sure,' Harley said tiredly as if his anger had taken all his strength. He sat down heavily in the chair by the desk and gave her a disinterested glance. 'Are you going too, Emily?'

Slightly taken aback she did not reply immediately. The room seemed to have grown very large and Harley had become a man she did not know. She said awkwardly, 'I will leave if that's what you want, Harley.'

He nodded absent-mindedly. 'It's time I fixed things up with your aunt. I will go tomorrow and see if she's well enough to travel.'

'So soon?' Emily bit her lips in distress. 'I thought it would be more fun for us after June has gone.' She moved closer to him and looked at him pleadingly. 'You do want me to stay, Harley?'

'Sure. Don't be upset, honey. I was thinking of you. There would be talk if you stayed here with me.'

She frowned. 'Gossip drove me here. Can't I ever get away from it? Can't I ever do anything right?'

'I don't want to discuss it now, Emily,' he said wearily, 'How about straightening up this room? The beds can be stripped and pushed back to the walls. We haven't any patients at the moment.'

Emily sat down on the nearest bed and burst into tears. 'You don't want me, Harley,' she sobbed, 'no one wants me. I might as well do away with myself.'

She was working herself up into a hysterical state and Harley stared at her in consternation. Swiftly he moved to her side and sat down beside her. 'Don't be so darn foolish,' he drawled softly. 'I've enjoyed having you here. But this is no place for a lovely young girl. You need more than this. Hush now, don't cry. When you've had time to think you will see that I'm right.'

She turned and buried her face against his chest. He put his arms about her and although his eyes were compassionate his face looked grim.

The door suddenly opened and June stood there. Harley did not move and stared at her over Emily's golden head with an inscrutable glumness.

Taking in the situation swiftly June said coolly, 'Sorry, I didn't mean to intrude. I will come back later.'

'Stay now you're here,' Harley spoke sharply.

Emily raised her head. She had ceased weeping but her face was flushed and her eyes blurred with tears. 'Don't go on my account, June,' she said shakily. 'I can make myself scarce.'

'There's no need for you to go, Emily,' Harley said firmly. 'June can wait for me in my surgery.'

June hesitated then said doubtfully, 'I wouldn't have come but Andy told me you wanted to see me.'

'That's right, I do. Go to the surgery!'

June nodded her head, then with lips pressed tightly together, she walked by them keeping her eyes well beyond them. If she had needed an incentive to go she had one now. It was the first time she had actually seen Emily in Harley's arms. Her heart felt heavy with regret as she entered the surgery. She waited, steeling herself to behave with dignity, praying that she would not reveal the pain which was attacking her so relentlessly.

When Harley entered the room and closed the door after him he had his anger well under control. But his lips had a bitter, sardonic twist to them and his eyes were bleak and condemning. June gave him a quick glance then looked away fear rapidly overwhelming her despair.

'Well, Nurse Bentley, what have you to say for yourself?' Harley remarked icily. 'I thought I was in charge here. What reason made you go over my head? I suppose you have notified Mr Burleigh that you intend to leave here?'

'Yes. I wrote to him,' June said in a subdued voice.

'Why didn't you inform me first?'

June moistened her lips. 'I was going to tell you today.'

'Real considerate of you,' he retorted sarcastically. 'That gives me a heck of a lot of time to replace you! Didn't you consider me at all?'

'I thought Mr Burleigh would see to that. Surely he would send someone to replace me.'

Harley muttered gruffly, 'No one could do that.'

'I'm sorry, what did you say?'

'Nothing.' He shrugged his broad shoulders. 'Why all the rush? Couldn't you have waited a few more weeks?'

'I told Chris I would go with him.'

'You think that's the best thing for you to do?' He was staring at her intently.

'Yes.' June clasped her hands tightly behind her and gazed at him unflinchingly.

He turned away. 'Is there nothing I can say which will make you change your mind?'

June closed her eyes fighting to hold her composure. She saw Emily's flushed face, Harley's hands caressing the girl's golden hair and said flatly, 'No.'

'Okay! If it's so important to you, go!' There was such a savage note in his voice that she started. Then after reflection she told herself he was angry because she had walked in on that tender scene, perhaps had interrupted a proposal of marriage. Also he was furious because she had not told him she was leaving. Harley was a proud man and he would not want Guy to be the first to know. She was at fault she knew. Had things been different she would have made a point of telling him first.

She said cautiously, 'I believe the plane is due in the day after tomorrow. With your permission I would like to spend today saying, goodbye, to the men. There are quite a few I would like to see and as they come into camp at different times it may take some time. Then tomorrow I can get my things together and tidy up here. I would prefer to leave everything in order.'

'You can please yourself what you do.'

Harley spoke with an effort. 'Has your brother gone back?'

'Yes. He didn't argue about my decision.'

Harley cast her a grim look. 'He's prejudiced. There's no need to prolong this interview, Nurse. I've said all I'm going to say.'

Her face pale and tight with suppressed emotion June said quietly, 'I've enjoyed my stay in the camp, Doctor. I do appreciate what you have done to make me feel at home. It couldn't have been easy, especially when you didn't want me here.'

'That's forgotten,' Harley said gruffly. 'I wish you well in your new life. My only fear is that you will regret your hasty decision.'

June nodded, turned stiffly and made for the door. She entered the clinic, hesitated, then rushed into Emily's room standing with her back against the door whilst she fought back the tears behind her burning eyelids.

There was no sign of Harley when she came out. The door of his surgery was open so too were the doors of the Mission and the fresh breeze was whisking the papers off the desk and scattering them in all directions.

June closed the doors and tidied the room. She stripped the beds and pushed them back out of the way then returned to the clinic to clear up in there. She was thankful to be alone for she needed time to adjust herself after that painful interview with Harley.

CHAPTER SEVEN

As Emily did not return before lunch June went across to the canteen on her own. She was rather surprised because there were so few places where the girl could have gone. She half expected to find her in the canteen but after a quick glance around discovered that she was not there. The doctor was not there either and it was some time before she learned from one of the men that Harley had left camp to attend to a minor accident case in another outfit and had taken Emily with him.

Try as she might to regard this as trivial June found it difficult not to feel slighted. She was Harley's assistant and it would have been natural for her to have gone with him. June felt rather lost as she listened to the men around her. If there had been a seat vacant near Chris she would have sat with him but he had come in much earlier and all the seats close to him were taken. Not that Chris seemed perturbed at not being with her. Since he had been on his feet again he had opened up a little and did not seem to mind being friendly with the men. They bore him no grudge now that they knew he was leaving and few of them mentioned the reason why he was no longer a crew boss.

With nothing much to do June found the afternoon and evening dragged although there was a little excitement in the canteen when she arrived for supper. The men had discovered that she was to leave on the next plane and bottles of wine were placed on the tables so that they could drink her health. If she had not felt so unhappy and depressed she would have been delighted to see that they thought so much of her and were going to such trouble to show their appreciation.

Emily and Harley had not returned when

June went back to the Mission House. To keep herself occupied she gathered up the personal items she had left in Emily's room and packed them away in her case. Then feeling that she might as well finish the task, she packed nearly everything else, turned out the lamp and went to bed. She fell into a deep sleep and did not stir when Emily, coming in very late, crept by to go to her room.

June awoke early the next day and reminding herself that it would be her last one at Smoky River decided to make the most of it. She washed, pulled on slacks and a bright blue sweater and went for a stroll before breakfast. She met Chris on her way back and was surprised when he greeted her with more enthusiasm than he had been showing recently.

'Our last day, June! Aren't you excited?' he asked as he strolled through the bush with her.

She glanced at him uncertainly. 'Not really. I shall be sorry to leave.'

'It's not been too bad for you but I've been counting the days. I couldn't have stayed another week.'

'I know. These last few days have been trying for you. But I thought you were feeling more contented. You appear to be friendly with the men.'

He smiled wryly. 'On the surface perhaps. They know and I know that nothing is changed. They don't like me and I'm not too keen on them either.'

'It's a great pity. You are so good at your job.'

'There are other places. I rather fancy a spell in West Africa. I could have gone there instead of coming here.'

'Do you blame me for that?' June asked quietly.

'No. It was Andy who persuaded me. If I had refused to come would you have stayed behind with me?'

June shook her head. 'To be quite honest I think I would have come with Andy. I was fond of you Chris but not enough to part with Andy. It was only after we got here that I thought I cared for you enough to marry you.'

'Now you realize I was right. You don't love me. I sensed all along that you didn't.'

June frowned. 'I was very sure before I left Vancouver.'

'You had known me so long. It was mostly because you needed someone. You were lonely. I guess it was the same for me. Then I became totally involved in my work and I knew that you would never mean as much to me.'

'Thanks,' June said suppressing a rueful smile. 'I wish you had made that clear before. You caused me a lot of un-happiness. Why didn't you tell me you wanted to break with me? Andy's hints were all I had to enlighten me.'

'I didn't want to hurt you. I thought I could do it gradually.'

'You were afraid I was going to cling on to you.' June said bluntly.

'Yes I did.'

'It was an unkind way of doing it. A girl would rather be told outright that she's not wanted.'

Chris frowned. 'It wasn't like that. I was rather unsure myself. I had a suspicion that if I broke with you I would regret it. It was stupid the way we rushed into an engagement. Neither of us was ready for it.'

'Yes I can see that now.'

'I appreciate you coming back with me. I hadn't expected that. In some ways I wish ...'

'Now don't spoil things. You know you will be happier on your own in future.'

'I feel responsible for you. You would never have come here but for me.'

'I don't regret that. I've enjoyed it.'

'Then why are you leaving? No, you needn't answer that. I can guess. It's because of Tretton isn't it?'

June gave him a startled glance. 'What makes you think that?'

221

'I've noticed the way you look at him.' He smiled. 'I've had ample time to watch all of you. If it wasn't for Emily I think he might become interested in you.'

June turned her face away. 'I think you are wrong and I would rather not discuss it. Do you intend to stay in Vancouver for awhile?'

'No. I've got enough cash for my plane ticket. I shall go as soon as I've reserved a seat. There's no point in hanging around. I haven't enough money for that.'

'You will be careful of those hands, won't you?' June said anxiously. 'You nearly lost the use of your fingers. Doctor Tretton was so skilful that he saved you from being unable to use your hands. It would be a great pity to damage them now. When you are in Vancouver do go to hospital and have them examined and please keep them bandaged and protected.'

'You don't have to remind me. I'm fully aware how much I owe the doctor. I can't understand why he buries himself up here.

Emily told me he is a surgeon.'

'I believe so.' June hastily changed the subject. 'I'm feeling hungry. How about you? Shall we go to early breakfast?'

Harley was coming out of the Mission House when they returned from the canteen. He was not in a pleasant mood and did not wait to speak to them. Chris went off to speak to a man he knew and June hurried into the waiting-room. There she found Emily humming to herself as she combed her hair in front of a wall mirror.

'You sound pleased with yourself,' June commented.

Emily turned round and said gaily, 'I feel reprieved! Harley was going to take me to my aunt's today but something's wrong with the jeep so we shall have to leave it until tomorrow.'

'Oh? I didn't know. Is Harley taking you back because I'm going?'

'Something like that. It's crazy isn't it? He thinks there would be gossip.'

'I expect there would be.'

'I wouldn't care if there was but Harley's different. He worries about things like that.'

'You ought to be grateful. It shows he thinks a lot of you.'

'Oh sure. But it doesn't make sense to me. You stayed here with him and no one gossiped.'

'That was different. I'm his assistant.'

Emily said shrewdly. 'There could be another reason.'

June frowned. 'You think there was some talk when I came?'

'No. Harley might be fed up with me. Perhaps he wants to get rid of me just as my folks did and my aunt did.'

'Nonsense!' June smiled at her stricken face. 'Forget the unkindness, Emily and be happy.'

'I shall miss you June,' the girl said wistfully. 'It's meant a lot to me having you to confide in.'

'We can write to each other and perhaps one day we could meet. I intend to get another post in Vancouver. Do you ever go there?'

'Sure. I've been there with Dad. Perhaps Harley will take me when he has a vacation.'

'Well, don't insist,' June said hastily. 'There will be heaps of time to decide what you are going to do. Your aunt will be going to Grande Prairie soon. You will go with her won't you?'

Emily looked doubtful. 'Only if Mom says I can go back.'

'I expect the gossip about you and Herbie has blown over by now. People soon forget.'

'Maybe. I wish I could. If Herbie walked through that door this minute I would rush into his arms.'

'That wouldn't be quite fair would it? I mean you do owe Harley some loyalty.'

Emily shrugged her shoulders. 'Herbie isn't likely to come so there's no point in tearing myself in two. I'm lucky to have Harley.'

'Yes you are.' June said quietly. 'I've got one or two things I want to do then I'm going to finish visiting the men. Do you want to come with me?'

'Sure. Can we have a swim first?'

'I don't see why not. It's a lovely day. It's going to be hot.'

The time passed all too quickly for June who wanted to savour every minute of it. She might have enjoyed it more if Harley had been more friendly but it was obvious that he was keeping out of her way and when she did meet him he was so cool and distant that she was relieved when he found something else to do.

The plane was due in at eight o'clock the next morning and would leave soon after so June went to bed earlier than usual. She was the first to awake and went into the waiting-room to shake Chris and inform him that it was six-thirty, the time they had arranged to get up. Then she returned to the clinic to dress in a dark green trouser suit and white silk blouse. She packed the remainder of her things and when she had finished joined Chris in the canteen for breakfast. He also was wearing a suit, shirt and tie and looked strangely out of place amongst the oil-men's outdoor garb.

'Eat as much as you can,' June advised him. 'It may be sometime before we have another meal.'

'I feel too excited to eat,' he said smiling at her. 'I thought this day would never come.'

'After awhile you will forget you've ever been here,' she remarked as she poured maple syrup over the flapjacks.

'Not until these are healed,' he said looking at his bandaged hands.

'Oh, I'm sorry. Do you need any help?'

'I can manage. Don't fuss, June.'

'Sorry, I forgot. You're not my patient now.'

The door opened and Harley came in. He was wearing a bright, yellow sweater and dark slacks and looked much smarter than he usually did at this time of the day.

His eyes held June's for a brief second then he nodded unsmilingly and walked by her, taking a seat farther down the table. Emily came in a couple of minutes later looking very sweet in a blue silk dress and a long white cardigan which was fluffy and feminine. June thought she appeared much older then realized that it was her hair style. Instead of having it loose about her shoulders she had pinned it up close to her head.

She smiled at June then passed by to join Harley who was frowning darkly at the men who were whistling at the girl.

Chris said idly, 'It looks as if the doctor is taking Emily out for the day.'

June did not answer him pretending an interest in her food which she did not want. The sight of Harley's powerful figure had reminded her of all she was about to surrender. I did see him every day, she thought sadly. After this morning I may never see him again. She swallowed hastily and pushed her plate away too stricken to try to eat any more.

'I knew you wouldn't have room for all that,' Chris said. 'If you are finished we might as well go.'

'Yes.'

Chris got to his feet and walked to the door. June hesitated with her eyes on Harley and Emily. She could not go without speaking to them although she knew that it might be easier and safer for her own sake. But Harley was gazing at her and she felt compelled to move towards him.

She smiled faintly. 'Chris and I are going now. I hope you like your new assistant, Doctor. Good-bye, Emily. Have a good day.' Her voice sounded brittle and much too bright.

Harley got to his feet. 'Do you intend to stay in Vancouver for awhile? If you do see that Chris gets his hands attended to.'

She nodded. 'I will. Good-bye, Harley.' She did not look at his face as she shook

229

hands with him and turned away before he had finished wishing her a good trip. Moving swiftly to the door where Chris was waiting for her, she stumbled down the steps into the fresh morning air and welcomed the coolness to fan her feverish cheeks.

'Harley said his farewell to me this morning,' Chris explained. 'He looked in for a few minutes whilst you were dressing. I believe he wanted to see you but I told him you weren't ready.'

'It doesn't matter,' she muttered. 'I hate prolonged farewells. I'm glad it's over.'

But she could not rid herself of a deep disappointment. Why she did not know. Harley had been very friendly. He had not been caustic or mocking as she had half expected him to be.

A haze of heat was shimmering above the tops of the pines and it would not be long before the sun penetrated the clouds and soaked the camp in brilliant sunshine. I do wish I could stay, June thought wistfully as she walked across the sandy earth to the Mission House with Chris. They had to take their luggage out to the truck which was waiting to take them to the air-field. And they would be gone within half an hour. Against the solid green of the forest the painted Mission House stood out sharply. Strange but it's never seemed so vivid or so beautiful, June mused. The day is doing its best to make the leaving memorable.

Chris said very little as he carried his gear out to the mail truck and was too preoccupied to notice how subdued June was. But squeezed into the front seat between Chris and the driver of the mail truck June had little time to grieve. The driver chewed gum and made wisecracks unceasingly as he drove carelessly over the bumpy road. June was thankful that they had not far to go for her head kept hitting the roof of the truck whenever the vehicle struck a rise in the dirt road.

'Only you two going back this time,' the

driver drawled as he climbed down. 'It will be a small plane and the bush pilot will only stay a few minutes. I believe he's bringing in a couple of VIP's.'

The plane was late and when it did arrive the bush pilot grumbled to the mail man that he had been having engine trouble.

'You two the ones I have to fly back?' he asked Chris and June who had been listening with a few questioning glances at each other because neither relished the idea of using a plane with engine trouble.

When they nodded the pilot went on, 'I reckon you may have to kick your heels for awhile. There's one or two mechanical faults I have to have fixed first.'

'That's all right,' Chris said hurriedly. 'We don't mind waiting. Don't hurry on our account.'

The pilot walked off to talk to the mechanic who was stationed in camp and who had arrived on the air-field a few minutes before and June found her attention being drawn to the plane from which two men had alighted. As they walked towards her she recognized Guy Burleigh but the other man she had not seen before. She would have known him at once if she had for he was a strikingly handsome young man with a crop of very fair hair. He was younger than Guy about twenty-five June guessed and more expensively dressed. In fact his well creased slacks, white sweater and navy blue jacket looked as if they had not been worn before. He was swinging his shoulders as he walked and his self confidence was having a devastating effect on Guy Burleigh.

It took June a few seconds to recover from the shock of seeing Guy so sub-servient. He was usually so cocky and sure of himself. It amused her to see him behave in such a servile manner and she wondered who his companion could be. Someone very important, she decided, otherwise Guy wouldn't be looking so obsequious.

She had been bracing herself to meet

Guy, expecting him to ask a few questions; had been a little afraid to encounter his banter and was slightly astonished when he walked by without acknowledging her or Chris. That's the first time I've seen Guy behaving like an employee, she thought. How the mighty have fallen! But I do think he's overdoing it. He was positively fawning on that young man! What a pity I'm leaving. It would be interesting to see what happens in the camp.

A few minutes later the pilot beckoned to her to go across to the plane. Chris had wandered off and June hurried after him to tell him that they were ready to go. June had intended to ask the mail man whom the young man was but the pilot was looking annoyed and had already told them to get a move on. It was not until they had scrambled inside that the pilot's face brightened.

'Sorry about that. Nothing has gone right today but I didn't mean to take it out on you.'

June smiled as she watched him adjust his seat. 'Did you get the engine repaired?'

'They did what they could.' He switched the engine on and listened with a gloomy expression on his face. 'It's not right. There, can you hear it? There's a definite knocking. I reckon that VIP has given us a djinn. I wanted to ground the machine but Burleigh wouldn't hear of it. We shall be lucky if we get back in one piece.'

June glanced at Chris who was smiling. The engine sounded well enough to her but she did notice that the plane was vibrating fearfully.

'Don't worry, June,' Chris said. 'He's pulling your leg. Pilots don't like these small planes.'

The man turned his head and grinned at her. 'I didn't mean to scare you, Nurse. I'm letting her warm up before we take off.'

'Who was the young man with the fair hair?' she asked curiously.

'Son of the Senior Partner, no less. Guy

called him, Herbie. Herbie! I ask you! Isn't that some name for a VIP?'

June said quickly, 'Do you know his surname?'

'Aberhart. His father owns most of the shares in the Company.' The pilot was making ready to move. 'Hold on it may be bumpy!'

Herbie Aberhart! June's surprise was leaving her and she was aware of a surge of excitement as she recalled what Emily had told her. Could it possibly be the same Herbie? Emily's boy friend? If so Emily was going to have a wonderful surprise. Did he know Emily was there? Was that why he had come?

Perhaps it was fortunate that she had something to concentrate on for she missed the pilot's fierce ejaculation and look of alarm as he frantically grappled to get the plane to rise. And it was Chris who jolted her back making her conscious of their predicament.

'My God! We'll never making it!' he

exclaimed fearfully.

'You are right,' the pilot said tersely. 'I shall have to turn her. We shall crash, no doubt about it, so hold on, brace yourselves ...!'

June moved closer to Chris and glanced at his face. He was so pale that even his lips were colourless. Fear made her stiffen and bereft of thought she waited. A movement from Chris made her aware that he was trying to shield his bandaged hands and she instantly forgot the danger to herself.

'Hold them down, Chris,' she said in an agonized voice.

She did not hear his reply. The plane had turned at a steep angle and the ground seemed to be coming towards them swiftly. June threw herself across Chris covering his hands with her body. She heard him gasp at the pressure and that was the last sound she remembered.

The news that the plane had crashed into the trees spread quickly and the men poured from the camps and derrick sites near-by to reach the air-field. The bush pilot, dazed with shock, had crawled out from the entangled branches where the plane had embedded itself. Whether his passengers had escaped or not he did not know for the machine had broken in two and the rear part had crashed into the undergrowth.

The mail man steadied the pilot after he had jumped to the ground. 'Where are your passengers?' he asked anxiously.

The pilot looked back at the mass of twisted framework. 'I reckon they've had it,' he said tersely. 'It will go up in flames any minute. If you value your lives, keep away!'

Then the sound of a truck roaring towards them made them spin round. Harley was at the wheel and his face whitened as he saw the wreckage but he did not stop and drove well into the bush before he switched off the engine and climbed out.

'I need three men!' he shouted. Too many rushed forward and he waved them back after he had selected the ones he wanted. 'Get up into the back of the truck and hack away at that debris! The tools are there. Work fast!'

They found June first and handed her limp body across to the doctor in silence for they all assumed she was dead.

'She's breathing!' Harley unashamedly brushed the moisture away from his eyes then said gruffly, 'Take her, Pete. Careful how you handle her and see that she's made comfortable in one of the trucks. I will be with you shortly.' He turned back to see how the men were faring and his grim face lightened a little when he saw that they were easing Chris through the space they had prised open.

'Where's June?' Chris cried frantically. 'I can't leave her.'

'She's okay. We got her out,' Harley said.

'For God's sake get out of there,' the

pilot screamed at the top of his voice. 'She's going up!'

Swiftly the men lowered Chris to waiting arms and Harley realizing that he would not be able to drive his truck away in time ordered everyone away. With only seconds to spare they all reached safety. The plane which had been blazing fitfully suddenly roared into vivid flames and exploded.

Harley rushed to the truck where June had been taken and swiftly examined her. His eyes were bleak and his face taut as he instructed the driver to return to the camp. The two men in the truck did not dare to speak for Harley's fear had touched them also. June's colourless face beneath her auburn hair gave them no hope at all and secretly they thought Harley was being too hopeful. If they had but known it the doctor's anguish was far greater than their's for he fully realized that only a miracle would save June.

CHAPTER EIGHT

It was six hours before June recovered consciousness. Her first sensation was one of fear. Then she saw Emily sitting by her bed and panic receded. Everything appeared to be so normal. Emily was reading a magazine and sunlight filled the room. Why am I in Emily's room, she wondered and what am I doing lying in bed in daylight? Then she moved and instantly she remembered and understood. Panic attacked her again as the pain became acute and she closed her eyes fighting both. She felt sick with fear as she tried to speak and found it was impossible.

Emily had noticed a slight movement. She glanced at June and became frightened at her pallor. Throwing down her magazine she rushed into the surgery.

'Harley, come at once! June's recovered consciousness but she looks awful. I reckon you ought to hurry. She's real bad.'

'Okay, don't look so upset. She's a very sick girl.' He got to his feet and quickly entered the clinic and turned into the sick-room.

When June opened her eyes he had his fingers on her wrist checking her pulse rate. 'How do you feel?' he asked quietly. Then seeing that she was making an effort to speak without much success said soothingly, 'Don't talk just yet. Have a drink first.'

Emily handed him a glass of fruit juice and he spooned some of the liquid between June's lips. She smiled faintly then as he watched her intently muttered awkwardly, 'I can't talk. What happened?'

'You're doing fine. Your jaw took a knock. It's bound to feel stiff. Do you remember the plane crash? You are lucky to be alive.'

She closed her eyes and then opened them again. 'Chris?' she whispered.

'He's okay, and the pilot. There's nothing to worry about.'

'Why can't I move?'

Harley gently smoothed her hair away from her eyes. 'You cracked a couple of ribs. It will be painful but it's not serious.'

'My head hurts. I'm so stiff.'

Knowing that June would not be satisfied until she knew the extent of her injuries Harley said patiently. 'You have a gash at the back of your head. I had to cut some of your hair. And you had so many cuts and bruises I had to bandage you up pretty thoroughly. That may be why you feel stiff and ache so much.' He looked at her anxiously. 'I'm going to give you a sedative. Sleep is your best medicine. But if you do wake, Emily will be here and I won't be far off. Try not to worry.'

Harley felt a little happier as he went back to his surgery. June's state of deep insensibility had worried him for he could not be certain how much damage the blow on her head had done. She might never have come out of that coma. That she had done so and had been able to speak lucidly afforded him great satisfaction and relief. Now with careful nursing she would recover with only a few scars to remind her of the crash.

It was nearly ten o'clock before June awoke. She felt much better for her head no longer throbbed so painfully and she was able to bear the acute pain of her body when she tried to move. Now that she knew what was wrong with her it did not seem so frightening.

'Try to keep still,' Harley said, frowning when he heard her gasp. 'Does your head ache much?'

'No. That seems all right.'

'Good. I can give you something for the pain. I hope you are going to be a reasonable patient.' He smiled at the flash of indignation in her blue eyes.

'That depends on how long I shall be one.'

'You ought to know the answer to that. It's foolish to rush things.'

'Where's Chris?'

Harley's jaw tightened and his eyes became steely. 'He has left. Guy had another plane sent up. Chris didn't want to hang about once he knew you were going to be okay.'

June closed her eyes seeing again those last few minutes before the crash.

Harley who had been watching her worriedly said gruffly, 'He asked me to thank you.'

Her long lashes flew up and she stared at him blankly. 'What for?'

'Chris said you saved his hands by throwing yourself across him. I guess that's how you got that gash on the back of your head.'

June smiled. 'It was worth it. I'm so glad about his hands.'

Harley said with a hint of fierceness, 'It

was a pity he didn't wait to thank you himself.'

'He had to get away. I know how he felt.' She was silent for a few moments then asked curiously, 'How was Mrs Rowley?'

'I don't know. We never got there. We had only driven a couple of miles when Emily asked me to turn back. She had forgotten the food the cook had given her for her aunt. I was annoyed at the time but thankful later for we were coming into the camp when we heard your plane had crashed. We drove straight to the air-field and got there seconds after it had come down.'

'It was lucky for me that Emily forgot.'

'It sure was,' Emily said eagerly unable to keep silent any longer. Harley had told her not to talk to June. 'The pilot was going to leave you. He thought you and Chris were dead and he was sure the plane was going to catch alight. Harley drove a truck close to the debris and he and some other men hacked away until they found you.'

June's eyes were dark with shock and incredulity, 'So, you saved my life!'

'Perhaps. Someone would have got you out. Don't dwell on the accident.' He frowned at Emily.

June muttered in a frightened voice. 'Is there some thing you haven't told me? What's wrong with my legs?'

'Nothing, absolutely nothing! I've told you the extent of your injuries and I wouldn't have done that with any other patient. Don't you trust me?'

'I'm not sure,' June said slowly. 'My legs feel heavy.'

'Bandages, that's why. For Pete's sake stop imagining you are worse than you are! Why if you go on improving like this you will be up in a few days.'

Her eyes brightened. 'So soon? Then it's not serious.'

'Haven't I just told you!' He smiled and gently pressed one of her hands lying on the top blanket. 'It's a well known fact that nurses and doctors make the worst patients. You know too much, Nurse. Be thankful that you have no broken limbs.' He gave Emily a stern glance. 'Stay with her and don't answer her questions. In half an hour she can have something light to eat. I will bring it over from the canteen.'

June closed her eyes when he had gone. She did not want to get Emily into trouble and a few minutes later she fell into a deep natural sleep. When she opened her eyes it was night and the lamp had been lit. Harley was standing by the bed looking down on her.

'How do you feel now?' he asked.

'Heaps better. The nausea has gone.'

He nodded. 'The blow on your head was responsible for that. You were concussed I guess. That pretty green colour on your face when we carried you in here confirmed it.' He smiled. 'I'm happy to tell you your cheeks are now an attractive pink hue almost normal. I'm real pleased with you. Are you hungry?'

'Not very. I would rather have a drink but not glucose and water.'

'Okay. It won't hurt you to go without.' He filled a glass with fruit juice. 'Raise your head and take a good drink. Easy now, I will take the weight. Don't move more than you have to.'

Even that slight movement was exhausting and Harley dabbed her damp forehead with a soft towel after he had removed his arm from her shoulders.

He cast a professional glance at her. 'Are you warm enough? Anything else you fancy?'

'No thanks. Does Andy know?'

Harley chuckled. 'Everyone for miles around has heard. There's been a long queue at the Mission House door all day. You are a popular girl. I sent word to Andy and told him not to visit you yet.'

'Did you hear if Chris arrived safely?'

'Yes, he's safe.' Harley's face tightened.

'No more talking. Try to sleep. I shall be here if you want me.'

His presence was comforting. June dozed; opened her eyes once or twice then reassured by his big form sitting in the chair near the bed closed her eyes and finally fell into a refreshing sleep. He was still there when she returned to the dim light of early morning and was at her side when she attempted to move.

'There's no need for you to stay,' she said faintly. 'You look tired.'

'That's the least of my worries.' He smiled twistedly. 'I can see you are better. I do need a shave and a change of clothes. I will send Emily into you.'

A sleepy-eyed Emily came in a few minutes later. She had hastily pulled on a pair of jeans and a sweater and had not stopped to brush her hair. June was grateful for her help for it was less embarrassing to have the girl wash her and comb her hair. It was impossible for June to raise her arms and her breathing was painful.

Harley stayed with her again the next night. He had snatched a couple of hours sleep during the day and was looking less weary than he had done the night before. June thought he seemed dispirited and reminded herself that it was not surprising. She had been a source of annoyance to him from the very beginning. I bet he can't wait to get rid of me, she thought bringing a rush of tears to her burning eyelids. Unfortunately she could not brush them away and he noticed immediately.

'What is it?' he asked in alarm. 'Is it your head?'

'No,' she murmured making an attempt to smile. 'I was being silly, feeling sorry for myself. Please take no notice.'

'You know I can't do that,' he said gruffly as he gently dried her tears. 'I wish I could help, June. It's not the discomfort that is distressing you, is it? Are you afraid Chris won't wait for you?'

'It's not that.' Afraid that he might probe deeper she asked quickly, 'What happened

251

to the young man who came with Guy? I meant to ask Emily. The pilot said his name was Herbie Aberhart.'

Harley looked surprised. 'You know about Emily and Herbie? He's still here. He came up to see Emily.'

'I'm sorry.' June said shakily. 'I ought not to have mentioned him.'

'Why ever not?' he asked giving her a puzzled glance.

June closed her eyes. It was the easiest way to end the conversation and she did not feel strong enough to trust herself to say the right thing. No wonder Harley had been looking fed up! Emily might not have told him why she had been sent away from home. It would be a shock to find out about Herbie.

Emily had evidently been warned not to talk to June because the slightest noise made the invalid's head ache and Harley wished to shield her from any excitement. Once or twice June tried to speak about Herbie but Emily shook her head and warned her that she was not to talk. And as the days passed June found herself becoming more and more depressed. Now that she was improving she saw little of Harley although he came in twice a day. But he was very professional did not stay long and appeared anxious to get away.

On the tenth day after her accident Harley said June could get up providing that she sat in the sick-room and amused herself with looking at magazines. As she had seen most of them before she soon became bored and when Emily came in to enquire how she was June kept her in conversation.

'I know you have been deliberately keeping me in the dark about Herbie,' she said with a faint smile. 'You can tell me now, surely? I did see him arrive so I know he's here.'

Emily's eyes brightened. 'I've been dying to tell you! But Harley insisted that I was to remain silent. He said I would over excite you and he didn't trust me in a sick-room. If I hadn't promised not to talk he wouldn't have allowed me to see you.'

'I realize it was none of your doing. What made Herbie come up here?'

'He came to see me. What did you think of him? Did you like him?'

June chuckled. 'I only saw him for a few minutes. I thought he was very handsome and extremely confident.'

'He's certainly that.' Emily said eagerly. 'Do you know something? He was real angry with his Ma for going to see my parents. And he told his Pa that if he interfered in his private life again he was going to take me across to America and set up home there. His Pa needs him in the firm because he's hoping to retire soon so Herbie sure scored his point.'

'What happened then?' June asked curiously.

'His folks called on mine and apologized. How about that? Isn't that something? I bet Mom was pleased. Now all the folks want

Herbie and me to go back and be married in town.'

June was silent for a second or two then asked quietly, 'Have you told Harley all this?'

'Sure. He was one of the first to know. I'm real sorry for him. He sure is a nice guy. If Herbie hadn't come for me then I would have settled for being a doctor's wife.'

'Did Harley ask you to marry him?'

'No. I guess we hadn't reached that point. I knew he liked me and I sure cared for him but these things take time. I had to get over Herbie. I couldn't stop thinking of him.' She glanced at June who was frowning. 'Are you and Chris going to marry soon?'

'No, it's too soon.' June hurriedly talked of something else. She did not want to discuss her personal problems with Emily. The girl chattered too much and her remarks could be blunt and tactless and June's nerves were on edge. She could understand why Harley had insisted on Emily keeping quiet about Herbie. He too would be feeling hurt and disappointed. She felt a little annoyed with Emily for treating him so casually. No wonder he had been acting strangely lately! It couldn't have been an easy situation.

Emily said cheerfully, 'The plane comes in tomorrow and Herbie and I will be on it. I didn't intend to go if you had still been in bed but now that you can get about there's no reason for me to stay.'

June said carefully, 'I'm very grateful for what you did, Emily. What about your aunt? Is she going with you?'

'No. I'm going to see her later on today. Harley will make the arrangements for her. She won't approve of Herbie, that's for sure. She never liked me and I don't see why I have to have anything to do with her. If it hadn't been for you and Harley I would have been real miserable. Herbie wants to see you before he goes back.'

June smiled. 'If that's the case I think

I ought to dress and make myself presentable.'

'It might make you feel better. I will bring him in this evening before we have our meal. Now if you don't mind I will be off. Herbie's borrowed Harley's jeep and he's waiting outside for me.'

June dozed most of the afternoon then at five o'clock went into the clinic locked all the doors and gave herself a wash down. It was marvellous to be able to do things for herself and when she returned to her room she enjoyed dressing herself in red slacks, a white silk blouse and a black sleeveless sweater. For the first time since her accident she applied make-up and arranged her auburn hair to her liking and felt well satisfied with the result. And when Emily and Herbie arrived back she was sitting in the Mission House waiting for them.

'You look real nice,' Emily cxclaimed.

'Thanks.' June smiled. 'It was good of you to lend me some clothes.'

'June lost everything in the crash,' Emily explained to the young man who was listening.

'I'm sorry to hear that. You will be compensated I can assure you. If you let me know the value of the items that were destroyed I will deal with it personally.'

'That is good of you, Mr Aberhart. Luckily I didn't have a great many things. I left a few clothes at the hospital in Vancouver. A friend is looking after them for me.'

'Can I have them sent up to you?'

June hesitated. 'I don't expect to be here much longer. Emily has offered to lend me all I shall require.'

Herbie glanced at Emily indulgently, 'My fiancée can leave most of her clothes behind. We can order new ones for her in Grande Prairie.'

'Oh, Herbie, you are good. Can I really order what I want?' Emily could scarcely contain her excitement.

He laughed. 'From now on you can have

what you want. Nothing too outrageous mind! I think I will come with you and help you to choose.'

June decided she liked Herbie very much. It was obvious that he was very much in love with Emily but all the same he was not seeing her through rose-coloured glasses. He was an intelligent and strong-willed man and would be sure to stop Emily from doing foolish things. She's a lucky girl, June thought as she watched them together.

They did not stay long for both of them were hungry and intended going across to the canteen for a meal. 'Why don't you come with us?' Emily asked June.

She shook her head. 'Not today. I may feel stronger tomorrow.'

'I will bring something back for you then,' Emily said before they left.

Not wishing to go back to her room June sat down on a chair close to the wall and leaned her head back. She looked very pale and fragile as she sat there. It had been an exhausting afternoon for dressing herself and talking to Emily and Herbie had taken more out of her than she had reckoned on. Her ribs were still painful and hurt when she raised her arms. I was silly to stay up, she thought. I'm not as strong as I ought to be.

The door was kicked open and Harley came in carrying a tray. He did not look too pleased at seeing her up and put the food down on the desk with a dark frown on his face.

'I didn't give you permission to dress,' he said curtly, giving her a severe look. 'When you've eaten this you are to go back to bed.'

'Very well,' she replied in a subdued voice.

He gave her a keen suspicious glance for he had expected her to argue. 'Has anything upset you? Emily said that she and Herbie had been to see you.'

'Emily annoyed me a little. I think she might have behaved more tactfully.'

'About what?' he asked in surprise.

'Nothing,' June murmured cross with herself for mentioning Emily.

Harley frowned. 'Let's have it! Something's eating you. I'm fed up with all this indecision. If you weren't so ill I would shake some sense into you!'

June looked at him in astonishment for she had never seen him so angry. He was white faced and taut and his grey eyes blazed with fury and frustration.

'Don't lash out at me because you've been let down,' she said sharply.

He turned and walked away from her and when he returned to her side his face was more controlled. And after contemplating her for a few seconds he said bitingly, 'It's high time you came to grips with yourself. You carry loyalty too far. Chris has shown you time and again what kind of man he is yet you still persist in dreaming of a future with him. You're an intelligent person. Can't you see he's only making use of you?'

261

'I don't want to discuss my relationship with Chris,' June said shakily. 'It's not your concern. Just because you're disappointed over Emily there's no reason to take it out on me.'

'I'm not disappointed with Emily!' He glared at her angrily. 'If you want to know the truth I'm glad she's going. Ever since she's been here she's caused trouble between us.'

June stared at him in bewilderment. 'I thought you and Emily liked each other.'

'Oh sure. She's another one who uses people.' He eyed her thoughtfully then speaking in a more rational manner said firmly, 'Now that we've dismissed Emily how about explaining your extraordinary behaviour. Do you honestly contemplate marrying Chris or have you been using him to hide your feelings?'

It was a shot so direct that June gasped.

Immediately he was at her side. 'For the love of Mike don't look so stricken,' he said savagely. 'I've half guessed the truth.

Don't tell me I've been wrong. I've felt such a strong tie between us at times. You see I've been in love with you almost from that first meeting but I didn't think I stood a chance.' He gripped her hands and found that she was trembling. 'I'm sorry. I guess I ought not to have startled you like that. You're not well enough for shocks.'

She laughed breathlessly. 'I can stand that kind of shock.' Her eyes were a vivid blue against her pink cheeks. 'I've been so stupid, Harley. I thought you were in love with Emily and it's quite true I did use Chris as a shield.'

Harley put his arms about her and drew her close. 'Why the heck didn't I make love to you before your accident,' he said hoarsely as he kissed her gently on the mouth.

June smiled. 'If you had I wouldn't have gone on that plane. I've been in love with you a long time.'

Harley sighed. 'How was I to know? You were so cool and collected. I've been miserable for weeks thinking you were in love with Chris. Then when he told me what you had done to save him I knew I had lost you.'

She chuckled then gasped at the pain. She had forgotten her injured ribs.

'Take care,' he said anxiously. 'You ought to be in bed.'

'Let me stay a few more minutes. I want to explain why I tried to protect Chris. The main reason was because I knew what infinite pains you had taken to make his fingers mend. I couldn't bear to think that you had made all that effort for nothing. Chris came into it also but only as a patient.'

'It was wicked of you to pretend you still cared for him,' he said resting his cheek against her hair.

'I didn't. You assumed I loved Chris. He and I were finished that afternoon at the Rowley's homestead.'

'So long ago!' he exclaimed. 'Yet you never told me.'

'At that particular time you weren't behaving very kindly towards me,' she remarked teasingly.

He smiled grimly. 'I was jealous of Chris.'

June stared at him curiously. 'But it was you who arranged that meeting.'

'I couldn't stand you being unhappy. I did it for you. I imagined at the time that it was only a lover's tiff.'

'It was much more than that,' she said with a rueful smile. 'Now I know how you felt I realize how difficult it was for you. You are a good man, Harley.'

He laughed. 'You wouldn't say that if you knew what dark thoughts I've been harbouring lately.'

'We shall soon forget all the unhappiness. There's no one to stand in our way now.'

'Only Guy.'

June looked puzzled. 'Are you suggesting he won't allow us to marry?'

'No.' Harley laughed. 'I was joking. As a matter of fact I reckon I've got the whip-hand over Guy. Herbie and I got along real well together. And whilst he was here I pointed out to him certain flaws in the set-up. It was a marvellous opportunity for me. I've never had such an interested ear before. Guy always fobbed me off with excuses. Now Herbie has promised to raise the age limit for the men. We shall have no more untrained youngsters risking their lives.'

'That's wonderful! How amazing it is that Emily's boy friend turned out to be such an important man. It might have taken you years before the Company listened to you.'

'It is mainly thanks to you. You brought Emily to the camp and looked after her. Herbie wouldn't have been so willing to listen to me if Emily had not told him how happy she had been here.'

'It was nothing to do with me,' June protested. 'It was you. Good heavens I had to listen often enough to Emily's praises of you!'

'Don't start another argument, woman!' Harley laughed and kissed her swiftly. 'It's that hair! I've never seen such a wonderful colour. It's unfortunate that it has a temper also. How long will it take to tame you?'

'Never I hope.' June smiled. 'It wouldn't be good for you to have your own way all the time.'

'If you are expecting me to leave Smoky River the answer is no,' Harley drawled, his grey eyes twinkling. 'On the other hand if you insist ... well ... I will go along with anything you say.'

June gasped then said breathlessly, 'I wish you wouldn't make me laugh. It hurts! You know I don't care where I am as long as I'm with you.'

He looked at her seriously. 'It's time I had a vacation. My home is in Edmonton. I would like you to meet my folk. We can marry there and return to Smoky River until the winter. We shall make a good team. Don't you agree?'

'Absolutely. Can we live in one of the cabins?'

'Sure. I may even get one built for you with a shower. How's that?'

'That would make everything perfect!' June sighed happily. 'It was the one thing I longed for.'

Harley's eyes twinkled. 'The only thing?'

'Not quite, I did exaggerate. Even with a shower I wouldn't stay here without you.'

'I should hope not! Now my dearest June you have to hurry up and get well so it's back to bed for you.' And before she had time to protest he swung her up into his arms and strode with her to her room.

'I'm going across to the canteen to fetch two hot meals. My appetite has returned.' He grinned down at her. 'How do you fancy a quiet dinner together?'

'Wonderful!' she smiled. 'The first of many I hope. Don't be too long.'

Harley bent and kissed her lightly on the forehead then left her. June closed her eyes with a sigh of contentment. It was almost too much happiness to contemplate all at once. To love and be loved was enough for the moment. This time there was no uncertainty. This time it was for ever.

The publishers hope that this book has given you enjoyable reading. Large Print Books are especially designed to be as easy to see and hold as possible. If you wish a complete list of our books, please ask at your local library or write directly to: Dales Large Print Books, Long Preston, North Yorkshire, BD23 4ND, England.

This Large Print Book for the Partially sighted, who cannot read normal print, is published under the auspices of

THE ULVERSCROFT FOUNDATION